WITCHES' BREW

MORGANA BEST

GLOSSARY

*S*ome Australian spellings and expressions are entirely different from US spellings and expressions. Below are just a few examples. It would take an entire book to list all the differences.

The author has used Australian spelling in this series. Here are a few examples: *Mum* instead of the US spelling *Mom*, *neighbour* instead of the US spelling *neighbor*, *realise* instead of the US spelling *realize*. It is *Ms*, *Mr* and *Mrs* in Australia, not *Ms.*, *Mr.* and *Mrs.*; *defence* not *defense*; *judgement* not *judgment*; *cosy* and not *cozy*; *1930s* not *1930's*; *offence* not *offense*; *centre* not *center*; *towards* not *toward*; *jewellery* not *jewelry*; *favour* not *favor*; *mould* not *mold*; *two storey house* not *two story house*; *practise* (verb) not *practice* (verb); *odour* not *odor; smelt* not *smelled; travelling* not *traveling; liquorice* not *licorice; cheque not check; leant* not *leaned; have concussion* not *have a concussion; anti clockwise* not *counterclockwise; go to hospital* not *go to the hospital; sceptic* not *skeptic; aluminium* not *aluminum; learnt* not *learned*. We have *fancy dress* parties not *costume* parties. We don't say *gotten*. We say *car crash* (or *accident*) not *car wreck*. We say *a herb* not *an herb* as we produce the 'h.'

The above are just a few examples.

It's not just different words; Aussies sometimes use different expressions in sentence structure. We might *eat a curry* not *eat curry*. We might say *in the main street* not *on the main street*. Someone might be *going well* instead of *doing well*. We might say *without drawing breath* not *without drawing a breath*.

These are just some of the differences.

Please note that these are not mistakes or typos, but correct, normal Aussie spelling, terms, and syntax.

AUSTRALIAN SLANG AND TERMS

Benchtops - counter tops (kitchen)
Big Smoke - a city

Blighter - infuriating or good-for-nothing person

Blimey! - an expression of surprise

Bloke - a man (usually used in nice sense, "a good bloke")

Blue (noun) - an argument ("to have a blue")

Bluestone - copper sulphate (copper sulfate in US spelling)

Bluo - a blue laundry additive, an optical brightener

Boot (car) - trunk (car)

Bonnet (car) - hood (car)

Bore - a drilled water well

Budgie smugglers (variant: budgy smugglers) - named after the Aussie native bird, the budgerigar. A slang term for brief and tight-fitting men's swimwear

Bugger! - as an expression of surprise, not a swear word

Bugger - as in "the poor bugger" - refers to an unfortunate person (not a swear word)

Bunging it on - faking something, pretending

Bush telegraph - the grapevine, the way news spreads by word of mouth in the country

Car park - parking lot

Cark it - die

Chooks - chickens

Come good - turn out okay

Copper, cop - police officer

Coot - silly or annoying person

Cream bun - a sweet bread roll with copious amounts of cream, plus jam (= jelly in US) in the centre

Crook - 1. "Go crook (on someone)" - to berate them. 2. (someone is) crook - (someone is) ill. 3. Crook (noun) - a criminal

Demister (in car) - defroster

Drongo - an idiot

Dunny - an outhouse, a toilet, often ramshackle

Fair crack of the whip - a request to be fair, reasonable, just

Flannelette (fabric) - cotton, wool, or synthetic fabric, one side of which has a soft finish.

Flat out like a lizard drinking water - very busy

Galah - an idiot

Garbage - trash

G'day - Hello

Give a lift (to someone) - give a ride (to someone)

Goosebumps - goose pimples

Gumboots - rubber boots, wellingtons

Knickers - women's underwear

Laundry (referring to the room) - laundry room

Lamingtons - iconic Aussie cakes, square, sponge,

chocolate-dipped, and coated with desiccated coconut. Some have a layer of cream and strawberry jam (= jelly in US) between the two halves.

Lift - elevator

Like a stunned mullet - very surprised

Mad as a cut snake - either insane or very angry

Mallee bull (as fit as, as mad as) - angry and/or fit, robust, super strong.

Miles - while Australians have kilometres these days, it is common to use expressions such as, "The road stretched for miles," "It was miles away."

Moleskins - woven heavy cotton fabric with suede-like finish, commonly used as working wear, or as town clothes

Mow (grass / lawn) - cut (grass / lawn)

Neenish tarts - Aussie tart. Pastry base. Filling is based on sweetened condensed milk mixture or mock cream. Some have layer of raspberry jam (jam = jelly in US). Topping is in two equal halves: icing (= frosting in US), usually chocolate on one side, and either lemon or pink on the other.

Pub - The pub at the south of a small town is often referred to as the 'bottom pub' and the pub at the north end of town, the 'top pub.' The size of a small town is often judged by the number of pubs - i.e. "It's a three pub town."

Red cattle dog - (variant: blue cattle dog usually known as a 'blue dog') - referring to the breed of Australian Cattle Dog. However, a 'red dog' is usually a red kelpie (another breed of dog)

Shoot through - leave

Shout (a drink) - to buy a drink for someone

Skull (a drink) - drink a whole drink without stopping

Stone the crows! - an expression of surprise

Takeaway (food) - Take Out (food)

Toilet - also refers to the room if it is separate from the bathroom

Torch - flashlight

Tuck in (to food) - to eat food hungrily

Ute / Utility - pickup truck

Vegemite - Australian food spread, thick, dark brown

Wardrobe - closet

Windscreen - windshield

Indigenous References

Bush tucker - food that occurs in the Australian bush

Koori - the original inhabitants/traditional custodians of the land of Australia in the part of NSW in which this book is set. *Murri* are the people just to the north. White European culture often uses the term, *Aboriginal people*.

CHAPTER 1

*O*ne discount pack of hipster lace briefs, one large caramel almond latte, one plane ticket from Sydney to Lighthouse Bay. That's all I had to show for my life, or to be precise, that's all I could afford after I sold my old car.

I was about to do what every girl dreaded—move back home to the relatives. I had no choice. My degree in Classical Literature hadn't exactly prepared me for the workplace. I'd worked as a temporary waitress, as a barista, selling tickets at a cinema, anything I could get, but the jobs were few and far between. I had done plenty of spells to get permanent jobs, but nothing ever worked. I'd wished more than once that I was like a Hollywood witch who could wave a magic wand and make things happen, instead of being a normal everyday woman who practised traditional witchcraft.

"It's only until you get back on your feet," I said aloud, and then averted my eyes as the taxi driver shot me a quick look in the rear view mirror. I had no idea how I would cope with moving from the big city to the tiny beachside town of Lighthouse Bay, a move made all the worse by having to live with my elderly aunts. To say they were as mad as hatters was putting it mildly. Still, their Bed and Breakfast business in the Jasper family ancestral home was crumbling, as no doubt was the house itself—if my memory served me correctly—and they had offered me a partnership in the business. They said they needed young blood.

The taxi driver didn't make conversation, which suited me just fine. I looked out the window at the narrow, winding road leading from the township of Lighthouse Bay to Mugwort Manor with dismay. This was a far cry from Sydney. Had I made the wrong decision? Had boredom ever killed anyone outright? I shook my head. No, I truly had no other options. I had been living on instant noodles, and had become so ill from lack of good food that I even had to take a daily iron supplement. I would have to put my best foot forward.

I directed the taxi driver to take me to the main house, not the cottages that my aunts rented out to paying guests. The driver deposited my suitcases on the side of the road and then drove off, leaving me standing there.

Mugwort Manor loomed before me, looking quite *Wuthering Heights* but without the doom and gloom. Well, maybe a little gloom, but there were certainly no English moors around here. The Australian sky was bright and blue, the air salty, yet the landscape in front of me betrayed no sign that the sea was nearby. The dark dormer windows seemed threatening somehow, as if some arcane creature was watching me through hooded eyes between the ancient drapes. Jasmine and ivy clawed their way across the face of the house, clinging to every fissure they could find.

Trees hung over the pathway, almost as if they wanted to tear at guests. The undergrowth was thick enough to conceal any manner of creature. In fact, was that a menacing growl I heard?

"Stop being fanciful," I said aloud. I had grown accustomed to talking to myself. I figured whoever said that talking to oneself is the first sign of madness had not lived alone for any length of time. Or maybe they were right.

The house looked the same as when I had last seen it some five years earlier, just before I lost my parents. I had been raised in the northern suburbs of Sydney, and only after my parents went missing while on sabbatical in Kyrgyzstan had I regained significant contact with my aunts. My parents' estate was tied up in all sorts of legal entanglements, and my lawyer said they would not be declared dead for another two years. I didn't want them declared dead at all; I hoped they would somehow turn up. The Australian government was not looking for them. No one was, and I myself did not have sufficient funds to go to Kyrgyzstan. Even if I did, I wouldn't know where to start. The situation was entirely hopeless.

At any rate, my parents had done their best to avoid *The Aunts*, as they called them, and had never told me why.

I uttered a few choice words and then struggled up the moss-covered flagstone path to the front door of Mugwort Manor.

A fresh sea breeze picked up my hair. I flicked the few strands out of my eyes and inhaled the heady scent of jasmine. Although Sydney was also on the ocean, the air was nowhere near as clear nor as fragrant as the pristine air of Lighthouse Bay. Mugwort Manor was close to the beach, a beautiful beach which stretched along the east coast of Australia. One section of beach was patrolled, and frequented by surfers, while the remaining, longer section was a designated off-leash dog beach. I was looking forward to long walks on the beach to preserve my sanity.

I paused as butterflies welled in my stomach, warning me of an upcoming event. I'd had this precognition since childhood, a foreknowledge that served to warn me both of something good happening and also something bad. Unfortunately, my life had been full of more bad somethings than good somethings. I had no idea what this was signalling, but given my track record, I supposed it wasn't going to be good. My right eye twitched. That always meant something bad was heading my way.

I decided not to ring the doorbell and alert my aunts until my belongings were sitting nicely outside the front door, otherwise I was sure mayhem would ensue. They were not the most organised people in the world. With that in mind, I stacked my suitcases out of the way. My aunts were likely to charge out the door and fall over them. Aunt Dorothy, for one, was clumsy and short-sighted. Just as my hand reached for the brass doorbell, I realised I had left my handbag by the road.

I gingerly walked back down the uneven flagstones—they were an accident waiting to happen—being careful going downhill given that it had obviously rained recently, and heavily. That wasn't unusual for these parts. Lighthouse Bay wasn't in the tropics, but in summer, thunderstorms were common most afternoons.

I retrieved my handbag from on top of a clump of kikuyu grass and turned to go, hesitating as the sound of a powerful engine roared behind me. As I turned, a silver Porsche screeched to a halt and splashed mud all over me.

A tall, dark, and strikingly handsome man jumped out of the car, presumably to apologise. At least, I think that's how he looked through the mud in my eyes. I gingerly wiped it out and then removed the mud from my mouth as well. The man was now standing in front of me. It was all I could do not to drool: that strong jaw line, eyes that brought to mind the colour of Homer's 'wine-dark sea,' his muscular body, the way he exuded raw masculinity.

He was wearing a leather jacket and a scowl. "Name?" he snapped.

"You splashed mud all over me!" I said angrily, my initial attraction to him vanishing in an instant at his manner.

"That's a long and unusual name." He raised his eyebrows.

I did not find the remark remotely funny, and the man hadn't even bothered to apologise. "What do you want?" I said, none too politely.

"Is this Mugwort Manor?"

By way of answer, I pointed to the partly concealed sign nearby.

The man looked at the sign, and then walked up the flagstone path to the door, ignoring me completely. I stormed after him.

I knew this was a big mistake. I wasn't a people person and I hadn't enjoyed any of my jobs in the hospitality industry, so how did I think I would cope with rude customers at the B&B? I assumed this man was a customer, but I reminded myself he could be anything. I just hoped he wasn't a debt collector.

The man was already pressing the brass

doorbell incessantly. "You need to give them time to answer," I said.

He ignored me and rang once more.

Aunt Maude flung the door open, looked the man up and down, and then spotted me. "Valkyrie!" she said with delight. She pulled me into a big hug. I managed to extract my head from her ample bosom only with some difficulty.

The man clearly wasn't accustomed to being ignored. He cleared his throat loudly, and said, "I'm Lucas O'Callaghan. I've booked."

Maude ignored him. "Dorothy, Agnes, Valkyrie's here," she called over her shoulder.

Dorothy appeared in the doorway. "Oh, Val, you've gotten taller." She was looking directly at the man.

I groaned. "I'm over here, Aunt Dorothy." The aunts did not look related to each other. Aunt Maude was happily plump, as she put it, with a shock of white hair, while Aunt Agnes was stick thin. Her hair was as red as a fire engine, and she wore red, bat-wing, thick-rimmed glasses. On the other hand, Aunt Dorothy wore no glasses at all, and that was a problem. Her hair was salt-and-pepper at the roots and sported masses of frizzy split ends. Her eyes were a piercing cornflower blue, as were the other aunts' eyes, but that was all they had in common.

Aunt Agnes pushed past Aunt Dorothy and the man. "Put your glasses on, Dorothy. Hello, you must be Mr O'Callaghan. You need to come inside and register." Her voice was harsh, but all three aunts hated men. I had never found out why— perhaps they were all jilted in their youth. I would have to address this if the business were to succeed. She continued in a kinder tone. "Maude, get Valkyrie's suitcases and take them to her room."

"Um, you said I could live in the Assistant Lighthouse Keeper's Cottage," I said hastily, following the aunts into the foyer. Mugwort Manor creeped me out, and the aunts' collective eccentricity was wearing.

At any rate, the foyer was a grand affair. The parquetry floor would have been quite something in its day, although the extensive wood panelling on the walls looked medieval. The wide panels next to the strong oak entrance door had once been glass, but were now boarded up with heavy oak wood panels to match the walls. The place somewhat resembled a fortress, albeit a heavily decorated one. Two identical bronze statues of women in Grecian drapes and mounted on fluted column pedestals flanked the door.

The room would have been impossibly dark, only for the skylight in the vaulted ceiling and the huge window high over the door.

"Nonsense, dear." Aunt Agnes looked at me over the top of her bat-wing bifocals. "You need to settle in first, and we have so much catching up to do."

"I'm used to living alone," I pleaded.

Lucas O'Callaghan made a sound that sounded suspiciously like, 'No wonder.'

"Did you have something to say?" I snapped.

He held up his hands in mock surrender. "Sorry, *Valkyrie*." His tone held more than a hint of derision.

"My name's Pepper," I said, exasperated.

"Her real name is Valkyrie," Agnes said primly. "It's her legal name."

Dorothy nodded. "I asked her mother to call her *Valkyrie Chooser of the Slain who Shall Enter Valhalla*, but she refused, for some reason."

I resisted the urge to scream. "Aunts, everyone else calls me Pepper. The agreement was that if I returned to help, you would call me Pepper, and I could live in one of the cottages."

"Have it your own way then, Valkyrie," Agnes said waspishly.

The man crossed his arms. "Ladies, can I just register and get out of here?"

And that was when a body fell through the skylight.

CHAPTER 2

*T*he man lay on the parquetry floor in a pool of stained glass, all beautiful and colourful, like some sort of Salvador Dali painting.

I wanted to look away, but somehow, I couldn't. My breathing came roughly, and I feared I would faint.

Lucas O'Callaghan rushed to the man's side and felt for a pulse, which was overly optimistic of him, from what I could see. Sunlight hit one of the green shards of glass and bounced happily around the room, rather an incongruous sight in the midst of a fatal accident.

Or was it an accident? What was the man doing on the roof in the first place?

There would be time for questions later. I

turned to my aunts, the three of them clutching each other, their mouths open in shock. "I'll call the police." I reached in my handbag for my phone, but stopped when I heard a voice. Of course, Mr Perfect was already calling the police. I gathered my wits. "Perhaps we should leave the room."

The aunts nodded, and I followed them from the vast lobby into the adjoining living room, a dark and dismal room, the very antithesis to an inviting space. After we all sat, my aunts on the same enormous couch and I on one at an adjoining angle, I forced my attention to the room. Anything to stop me shaking. I was shaking so much I was all but vibrating, and my breath was stuck in my throat. How would I ever whip this place into shape? The old brick fireplace was blackened, stained by years of soot. The air was thick and musty. I wanted to cross the room to the heavy lace drapes and fling them open, but my legs were jelly.

The room was stiflingly dreary, and I suspected that even if I were to open the drapes, it wouldn't make a significant difference. A thick, dark carpet covered most of the floor, seemingly draining what little light managed to filter into the room.

"The police will be here soon," the man said as he strode into the room and sat, uninvited, on an armchair. It was an old wooden antique, upholstered in beige and olive green stripes. It was also undoubtedly expensive.

"Not a good start to your vacation," Aunt Agnes said, clearly trying to make an effort. "We can't give you a refund." Okay, maybe not.

He waved one hand in the air in dismissal. "I don't require a refund. I'm not on vacation. I've just inherited the Ambrosia Winery." His words were as clipped as his manner. I could tell he was tense, but he was trying to hide it. I suppose he could be forgiven for that, given the circumstances. I just didn't like the man.

My aunts gasped and clutched each other. The electric jolt that ran through the air was tangible. Agnes recovered first. "But Henry's surname was different."

"Henry was my mother's brother, not my father's," he said patiently, too patiently, as if he were explaining to a child. There was more than a hint of condescension in his tone. "Hence I have my father's name."

It made no sense to me, but my aunts were nodding. Their faces were pale and drawn. They were staring at Lucas O'Callaghan with shock, and was that fear?

Agnes stood up suddenly. "I'll go outside and wait for the police," she said, but before she was halfway to the foyer, the doorbell rang.

Agnes picked up speed, and the rest of us followed her. I hung back a little, not wanting to look at the body.

A male police officer stood over the body and spoke into his phone, while a female police officer ushered us back into the living room. "I'm Constable Walker," she said. "All of you wait here for Sergeant Carteron while I have a quick look outside. Did any of you see anybody else around before the incident?"

We all shook our heads, and she walked away, after casting a hungry backwards glance at Lucas O'Callaghan.

Sergeant Carteron hurried into the room and introduced himself. He flipped open his notepad and asked us to identify ourselves. I at once noticed the good sergeant wasn't wearing a wedding ring, and he was awfully attractive. I thought it rather strange that I had seen two good looking men within hours of my arrival in a small town. I wasn't complaining, of course, and I must admit it was an idle thought to distract myself from the gruesome scene of minutes earlier. Still, I couldn't help thinking that while Lucas O'Callaghan had a most unpleasant manner, the sergeant did not appear to suffer any personality defects. What's more, he was talented; he was doing a good job getting my aunts to speak one at a time rather than over the top of each other.

"It's just like we already told you," Agnes said. "We heard the doorbell, and when we went out, our niece, Valkyrie, was standing there with this gentleman who had previously booked."

"And did the two of you arrive together?" The sergeant addressed the question to me.

I shook my head. "No, we've never met. I caught a taxi from the airport, and was carrying my suitcases to the door when this man arrived."

The sergeant turned to Lucas O'Callaghan. "Is that your car outside?"

"It's my hire car," O'Callaghan said. "I normally ride a motorbike."

Of course you do, I thought, while wondering if I had heard the sergeant's name before.

Constable Walker returned at that moment. "No sign of anyone outside," she said to the sergeant.

"The Forensics team will be here soon," Carteron said. "I didn't recognise the victim, so I doubt he's from around these parts. You're sure he wasn't one of your paying guests?"

"Quite sure," Agnes said abruptly.

The sergeant nodded. "Well, we'll know more once we have a positive identification. It seems strange that he fell through the stained-glass window in the roof."

That had to be the understatement of the century. The stained-glass window depicted, or rather *had* depicted, an image of a dragon slaying St George. My aunts had explained to me more than once over the years that our ancestors had been animal lovers.

The sergeant said something in a low tone to Constable Walker, but she was off in a world of her own, staring at Lucas O'Callaghan. Perhaps she was more susceptible to his animal magnetism than I was, because she couldn't seem to take her eyes off him. The sergeant had to repeat his question before she responded.

"How long before police will remove the, um, man?" Agnes pointed into the foyer as if there was some doubt as to what she was talking about.

"We won't have to shut down the business, will we?" Dorothy asked.

"I very much doubt that it will come to that,"

the sergeant said. "The detectives will be here presently. It will be their call, but my guess is that they'll just cordon off the lobby and you can go about your business. Just don't go anywhere near the crime scene."

"Crime scene?" Dorothy repeated. "You don't think it was an accident?"

I stared at her in shock. "How could someone accidentally fall through a stained-glass window?" Agnes asked her, mirroring my thoughts.

"Perhaps he was on the roof looking for a view of the lighthouse, or the ocean," Dorothy said reasonably.

"If you were wearing your glasses, perhaps you would have seen the full extent of his injuries," Agnes said, none too kindly. "He had bruises around his neck. He'd been strangled."

Dorothy's hand flew to her mouth, and she gasped loudly. She trembled violently, while Maude did her best to comfort her.

I silently berated myself for not looking too hard, but then again, I hadn't wanted to look at the body. I had assumed his injuries could be attributed to his fall through the skylight. After all, it was a two storey house and he had fallen through glass onto a hard parquetry floor, but there had been scratches, deep gouges even, on him.

What sort of weapon could do that? Some sort of bizarre pitchfork? I shuddered. No, it looked like he had been attacked by a wild animal. I knew male red kangaroos would attack if they felt threatened, and could inflict serious injuries, but there would hardly be any kangaroos on top of the roof. Besides, kangaroos rarely came into towns. Australians knew the legend of the Bushland Panthers, large black cats, sightings of which had been reported all over Australia for the past one hundred years, but I had never heard of one in this area. And surely those injuries were inflicted before the man was on the roof. Yet if they were, how had he managed to climb up there? And why?

I gripped the edge of the couch and forced myself to take a deep breath. These were questions for the police to answer, not me. Still, if there was some sort of legendary panther or giant angry bird attacking people and dropping them onto the tops of houses, then I wasn't too keen to stay in Lighthouse Bay, penniless or not.

"Has anything like this ever happened around here before?" I asked the sergeant.

"I was about to ask the same thing." The voice was Lucas O'Callaghan's.

Constable Walker walked over to him, and stood there, smiling at him. I almost threw up at the look on her face. Had she never seen a reasonably good looking man before? Her partner was strikingly attractive, so I wondered why she wasn't making googly eyes at him.

"No, nothing like this has ever happened before," she said. "This is a quiet little town."

The sergeant appeared discomforted, so I decided to press him for information. "You've heard of incidents like this before, haven't you?"

He shifted from one foot to the other. "I only recently moved to town, but no, this is certainly the first time anyone has fallen through a stained glass window to their death."

I felt he was avoiding the question, but I pushed on regardless. "Has anyone had that type of injury before? It looks like some kind of wild animal did it."

A slow red flush worked its way up the sergeant's face. "That's up to the detectives to investigate. I don't know how familiar you are with small towns, Miss Jasper, but there are only a few police officers here, all uniformed, and the detectives have to come from the nearest city."

I nodded. I didn't know that, but it made sense. I'd never had occasion to think of it before.

I looked up to see that the constable had taken Lucas away and was standing with him by the window. She was writing his contact details in her notepad. She was giggling and flirting, leaning against the window frame. To my surprise, he was not reciprocating in the slightest. I had taken him to be a bad boy; perhaps I was wrong.

As she leaned ever closer to him, he took a step backward.

"So do we have to wait here for the detectives?" Aunt Agnes said.

The sergeant appeared a little puzzled by the question. "You shouldn't leave the vicinity until you're questioned by the detectives, so I suggest you do stay in the house."

"I meant, is Mr O'Callaghan allowed to go to his cottage?"

The sergeant looked doubtful and hesitated before answering. "No, I'd rather you all stay here, together. If there is someone outside, and there probably isn't,"—he held up his hands in a gesture of reassurance—"there's safety in numbers. Mind you, I'm sure there's no further danger, but I'd rather leave it to the detectives to make that call. I want you all to remain in this room until you hear from the detectives."

"But I need a bathroom break," Dorothy complained.

"Me too," the other aunts said in unison.

The sergeant looked a little exasperated. "Do you need to pass through the lobby in order to get to the bathroom?"

The three of them nodded.

He wiped one hand across his brow. "All right then, but all of you go together. Constable Walker, would you stand at the crime scene while they're away?"

The constable frowned, clearly dismayed to be drawn away from Lucas O'Callaghan.

After she left, Lucas returned to his position on the chair. The sergeant turned his attention to me. "Valkyrie—if I may call you that?—what are you doing in town? Just visiting your aunts?"

"My name's Pepper," I said. "Please call me Pepper. I've actually moved back to town to help my aunts with their business."

"You have experience in the hospitality industry?"

"Um, no, I have a degree in Classical Literature," I said defensively.

His eyebrows shot skyward. "Oh, a useless degree," he said, and then his face flushed. "Oh, forgive me. I meant no offence. So this is permanent?"

I sure hope not! I thought, stinging from his unkind remark. Aloud I said, "Well, maybe permanent is going too far, but certainly for the foreseeable future."

The sergeant smiled. "Welcome to Lighthouse Bay!"

Was he flirting with me? Lucas cleared his throat, and I shot him a glance. He seemed amused. I glared at him by way of response.

"And Mr O'Callaghan, what are you doing here?"

"I recently inherited the Ambrosia Winery, so I'm staying in town until I'm satisfied that the business is running just how I'd like it to run."

I watched the sergeant's face carefully, but he did not show the surprise that my aunts had earlier. "So sorry to hear about your uncle. You can't stay at the property itself?"

Lucas shook his head. "No, there's only one house at the vineyard, the managers' house—a husband and wife couple—so I could hardly intrude."

"Quite so." The sergeant tapped his pen on his chin. "And you two didn't see anything when you arrived? Not another car, not a person?" We both shook our heads. "Nothing at all that was out of the ordinary, even something you didn't consider important?"

I shook my head again, and then remembered something. "There was something, but it was probably just my imagination."

The sergeant nodded encouragingly. "Go on."

"I heard growling in the bushes right next to me, just before Mr O'Callaghan drove up. It sounded like a wild animal. It was the sort of noise a possum makes, but this animal sounded a lot bigger."

Lucas flinched.

CHAPTER 3

I looked at Lucas O'Callaghan, but his face wasn't giving anything away. Did he know something? It seemed more than a coincidence that this bizarre accident had happened the very day that Lucas arrived. Still, he had been standing with me when the man had fallen through the roof, so obviously he wasn't the one who had done it.

The sergeant scratched his chin. "Could it have been a dog or a feral cat? Are you sure it wasn't two possums fighting? They sound vicious."

I shook my head. "Quite sure. I know the sound of possums fighting. It was that type of sound, but it sounded like a much larger animal."

"And you didn't see anything?" he asked again.

"No, but that was exactly when Mr O'Callaghan drove up. Have any animals escaped from a zoo or a circus, perhaps while being transported? The highway isn't far from here."

Sergeant Carteron shook his head. "I'm sure the detectives will check that out, but that would normally be called straight through to the local police, and there haven't been any such reports."

The constable walked back in, ushering my three aunts in front of her. I suspected they had pretended that they needed to go to the bathroom simply to get a closer look at the victim, although why they would want to do so was quite beyond me. They looked dishevelled and were breathing heavily, as if they had been doing hard exercise. Aunt Agnes's bright red hair was sticking out at all angles. Perhaps it was the shock.

The constable walked over to stand near Lucas. She scrawled something on a piece of paper and handed it to him. "Here's my home phone number. Give me a call if you remember anything else." I couldn't be sure, but I think she actually winked at him.

At that very moment, a sleek black cat appeared as if from nowhere. She walked over to sit in front of the fireplace, and then proceeded to lick her paws.

"Perhaps you should lock the cat in a room, away from the crime scene," the sergeant said. "We can't have a cat contaminating the crime scene."

"We can't lock her up," Maude said. "She doesn't live here."

"Who does she belong to?" the constable asked.

"She belongs to herself, of course," Maude said, raising her eyebrows.

"Well then, why is she in your house?" The sergeant was unable to keep the exasperation out of his voice.

"She comes over to watch the *Gilmore Girls* on TV," Maude said.

"And we feed her, too," Dorothy added.

I bent down to stroke her. "What's her name?"

No one spoke, so I looked up at the aunts.

"She hasn't told us," Dorothy said.

Oh gosh, I was in a mad house. Of course, I knew that my aunts were eccentric, but I hadn't remembered until now just how eccentric they were. The sergeant's phone rang, and he hurried to the door. I couldn't hear what the other party was saying, but I could hear noise outside. I assumed it was the detectives and the Forensics team arriving.

And I was right. Soon the foyer was bustling with activity. After five or so minutes, the detectives came into the room. Constable Walker had been with us the whole time, and she could still hardly take her eyes off Lucas O'Callaghan.

The detectives introduced themselves as Banks and Anderson. I had expected they would take us away separately and question us, but they didn't. They did, however, tell us that we would have to go down to the local police station and make a full witness statement at some point that day. They didn't seem to have any sense of urgency about it.

"I'd like you all to stay put for just a few more moments, please." Detective Banks nodded to his partner and to the constable, and they all left the room, the constable casting a longing glance at Lucas over her shoulder.

I at once turned to my aunts. "What on earth could've happened? Did you see his injuries? That wasn't just from falling through the roof. It looked like he was attacked by a wild animal."

"Now don't talk about such things in front of our guest," Agnes said firmly, nodding to Mr O'Callaghan. "I'll ask the policewoman if I can fetch us all something to eat and drink."

She hurried out of the room. I noticed that the

other two aunts were knitting furiously. The black cat had her eye on one of the balls of wool on the floor. I thought I would try to get some sense out of the guest. "Mr O'Callaghan, what do you think happened?"

"He was strangled, obviously." His reply was curt.

"Yes, I know," I said through gritted teeth. "I was asking why he fell through the roof."

"Your guess is as good as mine," he said unhelpfully. "What do you think happened?"

My aunts made an attempt to shush me, but I ignored them. "As nobody was meant to be working on the roof, it's a mystery that he was up there in the first place. It's also a mystery that he had those injuries—unless he was skydiving and fell from a plane, but there were no signs of a parachute, and he would have been, um, more squashed. It just seems to defy reason. Sure, he was strangled, but he had serious injuries, more than falling through glass should do. I can't think of a single logical explanation for it."

"Nor can I," Mr O'Callaghan said. "Perhaps the detectives will be able to come up with one."

"Are you still going to stay here?" Maude asked him from over her knitting. "Or will you stay at a different B&B? One without dead bodies, and things like that." Her voice trailed away uncertainly.

"I'm happy to stay here," he said, "although I think we should all remain vigilant. I don't want to scare anyone, but if there's some sort of wild animal on the loose, perhaps we should all make sure we keep our doors and windows locked and not go out at night."

"But this happened in broad daylight," I pointed out, "and you and I were standing outside the house at the very time the man must've been up on the roof." At that point, I realised that the man was likely being murdered right when we were on our way up the flagstone pathway. I trembled as a wave of dizziness overcame me.

Aunt Agnes hurried into the room with a large pot of coffee. "I've made some sandwiches, but the police told me to hurry, so I couldn't rustle up anything more substantial. I have lunch in the oven, but it isn't quite ready yet. I did bring a plate of Tim Tams, too." She looked at Mr O'Callaghan. "I noticed a hint of an accent, Scottish isn't it?"

The man looked rather put out. "Irish, actually."

"If you haven't been in Australia long, Tim

Tams are an Australian chocolate biscuit, quite delicious. Perhaps you Irish call them cookies."

"Thank you, but I've been in Australia for quite some time." He leant across and selected a Tim Tam.

I was ravenous. The food on the plane had been scant, so I grabbed a plate and heaped a pile of sandwiches on it, and proceeded to gobble them up. I looked up to see Lucas looking at me with raised eyebrows. "What's your problem?" I said through a mouthful of crumbs. "Haven't you seen anyone eat before?"

Dorothy butted in before the man had a chance to answer. "Now, Valkyrie, be nice to our guest. You don't want to frighten him away."

She was right. I had been rude to a guest, and I was here to try to grow their business. "I'm sorry, Mr O'Callaghan." It had been such a strange day —it was all so surreal. I wouldn't have been the least surprised to wake up and find that it had all been a dream.

He waved my apology away. "You must be hungry."

I stuffed another sandwich in my mouth and nodded.

Lucas leaned forward. "Do you drink the wine from my winery?"

All three aunts looked startled, as if they had been accused of some heinous crime.

"Well yes, it's a local brand," Dorothy said. "We like to support the local businesses."

"And your uncle gave it to us at a discount," Agnes added, "for our guests."

I was perplexed. "I didn't think you fed the guests. I thought you left breakfast food for them in their cottages, and that was it."

"There are several vineyards around here," Maude said, ignoring me, "but Henry's was the closest. You're going to continue growing the wine?"

Lucas nodded. "Yes, the business will continue as usual. There's quite a demand for that type of wine."

He looked at the aunts intently as he said it. They all nodded, their faces carefully blank.

I was quite sure there was some subtext I was missing, some nuance that was beyond my understanding.

Lucas continued his questioning. "Did you know my uncle well?"

Dorothy and Maude looked at Agnes, who

hesitated before answering. "Yes, just as well as we know any other business owners around town. Were you and Henry close?"

"Not especially." Lucas's manner was guarded.

Maude leaned forward. "How did he die, if you don't mind me asking?"

Lucas's careful mask slipped momentarily, but he was quick to recover. "An accident, when he was on vacation overseas."

Detective Anderson came back into the room before I could get any further insight as to what was going on, if indeed there *was* anything going on.

"The crime scene has been processed, and the exhibit has been removed."

"What exhibit?" Dorothy piped up.

"It's what we call the victim," the detective said.

Dorothy stood up. "Well, why didn't you say so?"

The detective flushed a little, and then said, "You're all free to go about your business, but you can't go inside the area surrounded by police tape. We'll need that for a couple more days."

I heaved a sigh of relief. "Valkyrie will show you to your cottage," Agnes said to the new guest. "Dorothy, go get the keys. Mr O'Callaghan, you'll find everything in order, but feel free to ask should you require anything from us."

Lucas shifted from one foot to the other. It was the first time I had seen him look uncomfortable. "I'd rather one of you ladies show me to my cottage."

Dorothy re-entered the room and handed me his keys. "Why?" she said.

"The three of us have things to do, so Valkyrie will show you to your cottage," Agnes said in a tone that brooked no nonsense.

"May I speak to you in private, Mrs. Jasper?"

Agnes was clearly put out, but nodded and followed Mr O'Callaghan into the foyer. They returned moments later, with Agnes wearing a scowl on her face. "Valkyrie will show you to your cottage," she said once more. "Valkyrie, it's the Atlantis-themed cottage. Come back as soon as you've done that, and have some lunch. It will be ready by the time you get back. You must be ravenous."

I was dumbstruck, wondering why Mr O'Callaghan was so insistent that I not show him to the cottage. Did he think I was going to berate him for splashing mud over me? It didn't make any sense at all. Still, my aunts didn't make any sense either, so I supposed I'd have to get used to this sort of thing.

Mr O'Callaghan shrugged, a dark look spreading over his face. "I'll just get my suitcases," he said. I nodded and followed him back out the door to his car. I looked at the key, and it had the number five on it. To my horror, it was the closest to the cottage that the aunts had promised to me, the Assistant Lighthouse Keeper's cottage. My cottage-to-be had been removed from its original place many years earlier and placed at Mugwort Manor.

"Follow me," I said. I took off at a pace, half hoping to lose him. Why was he so concerned about me showing him to the cottage?

I unlocked the door and held it open until he walked inside. I had hoped to be shown over the cottages in person before I had to show any guests around, but I had seen them many times in my youth.

As soon as I opened the door, my jaw dropped open. It was a bit worse than I had remembered. For some reason, the aunts insisted on cottages that were heavily themed. This cottage was called the *Atlantis Cottage*, but sported mainly a pirate theme. The walls were adorned with a particularly garish wallpaper of pirate flags, fake cutlasses, and cannons. As far as I could tell, the only nod to Atlantis was the appearance of space-age prints in frames.

I showed him the kitchen and the bathroom, and then walked into the bedroom to open the curtains. I winced when I saw the double bed. It was in the shape of a ship, complete with a ship's wheel as a headboard. Over the headboard in a chrome frame hung an illustrated timeline of all the shipping disasters in the Bermuda Triangle. "There's a lovely view over the hills from this window," I said, hoping to draw his attention to the only positive I could see. When there was no response, I turned around to see he wasn't in the room.

I hurried out, for a minute worried he'd been mauled by some sort of animal just like the victim. To the contrary, he was standing in the living room, his arms crossed, looking at a silver-framed photo.

"Is something wrong?" I asked him. "You didn't want to see the bedroom?"

"I'll see it soon enough," he said gruffly, setting down the photo directly in front of me.

It was a black and white photo of a beautiful young woman, her long blonde hair streaming in the wind. She was smiling at someone, I assumed the photographer—Lucas? "Your wife?" I asked before I could catch myself.

"Someone very dear to me. She couldn't come with me this time."

I looked at the photo again, and then forced myself to look away. "Is there anything else I can do for you?"

His face paled, and he took a step backwards. "No, you can leave now."

I was horrified to realise how he had taken my words. I tossed the keys to him and he caught them with one hand. "I hope you enjoy your stay," I said, doing my best to inject sincerity into my voice. I hurried to the door, the thought of a wonderful home cooked meal, one that I wouldn't have to pay for, beckoning me to the manor. As my hand reached for the door knob, he spoke. "You're leaving so easily?"

I spun around, confused. "What do you mean?"

He looked a little embarrassed. "Oh, nothing. Thank you."

I nodded, and shut the door behind me. My duty was over, and the police had removed the body. I breathed a sigh of relief. Now I could settle in, the only black spot over my existence being the murder. Surely the police were right—people would know if a lion or a tiger had escaped from a zoo. Besides, what sort of animal could climb onto a high rooftop?

I hurried to the back of the manor, and into the kitchen. There was no sign of the aunts, so I assumed they were in the dining room. I walked through to see them sitting there, clearly waiting for me. I stifled a laugh. The dining room looked like something from *The Addams Family*. In fact, the whole house did, for that matter. The furniture was antique, and the room was completed by an ornate antique pump organ. The room was largely wooden; well-maintained floorboards covered the entirety of the floor, and the walls were set with heavy wooden panels.

I took my seat at the table, next to Aunt Maude and opposite Aunt Dorothy. Agnes sat at the head of the table. I suppose that suited her, because she was something of a control freak.

"This smells delicious," I said.

Aunt Agnes nodded. "Tuck in, everyone. We need to keep up our strength. It's my signature kale soup. There are tomatoes, beans, potatoes, parsley and more, but it's entirely tasty. It's good for you, full of iron. Just what you need."

I was surprised. "How did you know?"

Agnes looked blank. "Know what?"

"That my iron levels are low. I have to take a supplement every day."

Agnes shook her head. "Isn't everybody low in iron these days, what with fast food and the like?" She tut-tutted. "That's what I meant. Now eat up, dear. And let's have some of this nice wine."

I declined. "It's a bit early in the day for me to drink."

The aunts exchanged glances. "Nonsense," Agnes said brusquely. "Think of it as an elixir rather than wine. It's full of vitamins and minerals, just what you need," she said again. She poured the wine into a beautiful crystal goblet, decorated with blood red inserts in the shape of a pentacle, and handed it to me.

There was no point arguing. I gingerly placed my lips around the gold rim and took a sip. It smelled of blueberries and chocolate and happiness, if that were even possible. "It's surprisingly good," I said, and all three aunts nodded their approval. "Aunt Agnes, if you don't mind me asking, do you know why that guest was so weird about me showing him the cottage?"

"He seems to be a little afraid of women,"

Agnes said. "Pass me the bread rolls, would you, Maude?"

I set down my wine glass. "What do you mean, afraid of women?"

Agnes shrugged one shoulder and took a sizeable gulp of wine. "He told me that women always throw themselves at him. He didn't want you to try to put him in a compromising position, so he wanted someone our age to take him to his cottage."

CHAPTER 4

I laughed, thinking she couldn't possibly be serious, but then it dawned on me that she might be telling the truth. "Are you joking?" I asked her.

"No, not at all." Agnes took a large mouthful of bread, chewed it, and then busied herself buttering another slice. "He said if you made advances to him, it would make his time here difficult."

"Why, of all the arrogant…" I managed to stop before I said some words that would make my aunts' hair stand on end. "He certainly has a high opinion of himself. That arrogant jerk! How dare he think that I would want to…?" I hesitated once more. My original opinion of him had been right.

"Come to think of it, that woman constable was drooling all over him. Did you find that strange?"

I addressed the question to Agnes, but Maude spoke up. "There's a shortage of handsome men in Lighthouse Bay, apart from Sergeant Carteron, of course, but he doesn't seem interested in Constable Walker. I think the sergeant took a fancy to you, Valkyrie. Anyway, the constable is probably too young to realise that she doesn't need a man. They're nothing but trouble."

I rolled my eyes. I hoped the aunts wouldn't start one of their usual rants against the male of the species. Although, having met Lucas O'Callaghan, I was beginning to think they were right.

Detective Anderson entered the room, startling me. "Please continue your meal, ladies. Until we know the identity of the victim, I was wondering if you could all leave here and stay with someone for a few days, perhaps a relative."

Aunt Agnes jumped to her feet. "Absolutely not!" she exclaimed. "We're running a business here."

Detective Banks poked his head around the door and shook his head. "They won't go."

Anderson nodded to him and wiped his brow,

before turning back to us. "It looks as if all your guests are refusing to leave, as well."

"Do you think we're in danger?" Aunt Agnes asked. Her voice held no trace of fear.

"I don't have enough evidence to answer your question, Madam," the detective said solemnly. "I only know that a murder has been committed in your home, and at this stage in the investigation, it's too early to know whether or not you're in danger, but common sense would dictate that you leave for a few days until we look into it."

All three aunts shook their heads. "It's not going to happen." Aunt Agnes took her seat.

The sergeant turned to me. "Miss, do you insist on staying in this house with your aunts?"

Agnes interrupted him. "Valkyrie was going to stay in one of the cottages, but given the circumstances, I think she should stay in this house, with us."

"Yes, absolutely. There's no question about that," the detective said firmly. "I'd ask you all not to leave the house after dark, and to stick together as much as you can."

I made to protest, but then thought it over. Homicidal maniac or my aunts? It was a tough choice. "All right then, I'll stay here," I said. "I wouldn't be able to sleep at all if I were living in one of the cottages, to be honest."

My aunts exchanged glances, clearly pleased with my decision.

"And we'll feed you up, Valkyrie," Dorothy said. "You've clearly starved yourself."

"Not out of choice," I muttered.

"I'll have one of the uniformed officers drive by Mugwort Manor every few hours, night and day, until we find out what's going on," the detective said. "I assume you have security here?"

"Yes, we do," Agnes said. "We'll be quite safe inside this house."

"That man wasn't safe in the house," I pointed out.

"He didn't die *inside* the house," Agnes countered.

"Well, I'll leave you ladies to it," Detective Anderson said.

Aunt Maude stood up. "I'll show you to the door. Valkyrie has had a hard day, her first day helping us in the business."

The detective nodded to us and left the room. I spread some vegemite on a crusty bread roll and consumed it greedily.

"Now don't you worry about a thing," Agnes

said to me. "You're not in any danger here. Just don't go outside without one of us."

I forced a smile, wondering what help one of my aunts could possibly be if we encountered whatever creature or human had attacked the man who had been recently lying on the parquetry floor not far from where I was eating now. I fought a wave of nausea.

Aunt Maude walked back into the room, and before she had even reached her seat, spoke. "So, Valkyrie, are you still doing your spells?"

I gasped and dropped my butter knife. "How did you know?"

"Your mother told us, of course."

I frowned. "I didn't know my mother knew."

"Mothers know everything," Aunt Maude said, and the other two aunts nodded.

"So do the three of you practise witchcraft, too?" I asked them.

"Of course, dear. We practise traditional witchcraft, just like you." Aunt Agnes produced her knitting from a bag on the floor. "We mainly practise knot magic. We weave our spells into our knitting. Now the question is, dear, have you had much success with your spells?"

"I've had mixed success," I admitted. "I did

spells that I'd find things on sale all the time, and that worked, and I was always able to find a parking spot whenever I wanted one, even in the middle of Sydney, but I always failed in two areas."

I looked up to see all three aunts leaning across the table, their eyes beady and glittering. "And what would those two areas be?" Aunt Dorothy asked me.

I had probably said too much, but there was no turning back now. "I did spells to find a nice boyfriend, but I never met anyone, and I did spells to get a job that I'd really like. The other spells I did always worked, even if I had to repeat them until they actually happened, but those two spells never worked."

I expected the aunts to say something philosophical, or to say I was better off without a man, but they did not.

"That's because you were going to find better options elsewhere. Just think, if you had found a job in Sydney, you wouldn't be here now!" Aunt Agnes's voice ended on a note of triumph.

I resisted the urge to say, 'That's exactly my point.'

"And that's why you haven't found a boyfriend," Aunt Agnes continued.

"Yes, men are no good," Maude said.

Aunt Agnes narrowed her eyes. "Hush, Maude! Valkyrie, the right man hasn't come along yet, not that you need a man. Well, you go and take a nice relaxing bath, and we'll attend to the washing up. You've had a long day, Valkyrie."

"Pepper."

"Quite so. Your room is the one you always stayed in when visiting us. Off you go!" Aunt Agnes shooed me away.

Before I had gone far, she called me back and thrust a tall goblet of wine into my hands. "Take this with you, and drink it, but sip it slowly. It takes some getting used to."

"Throw your clothes outside the bathroom door and I'll wash them for you," Aunt Dorothy called after me. "I'm about to do the laundry."

I walked up the staircase, wine goblet in hand, skirting the yellow police tape around the centre of the foyer. I averted my eyes from the scene, even though the victim's body was no longer there. I shook my head. What a strange beginning to my new life.

I opened the door to what was to be my new room for the next few days—I hoped no longer than that. I immediately crossed to the windows and opened the curtains wide. My aunts dreaded open windows, saying that people would look in, and that the sunlight would ruin their antique furniture. The aunts' bedrooms all looked over the front of the house, but this room looked over the back of the manor. It was a secluded location, so it wasn't as if people would look in at any given time.

I tied back the heavy gold brocade drapes with the golden rope tassels hanging at the sides. I made to open the tall sash window, and then had second thoughts. If a creature had dragged a man onto the roof, would it be able to get through my window? I shook my head, dispelling such fanciful notions. The person was clearly murdered by a human, not an overgrown angry wombat.

I flipped the latch and pushed the window upwards. It was a struggle, probably because it hadn't been opened in years, but to my delight, it opened fully. I looked around the room for something to hold it open. I didn't want to be the cause of the heavy sash window falling down and smashing. These things would be awfully difficult to replace, not to mention highly expensive.

I couldn't see anything, so instead took the five hideous cushions from the bed. They were all a faded beige tapestry and looked antique, not my taste at all. It took some doing, but soon I had them all wedged between the windowsill and the bottom of the window. Later, I would find a piece of dowel or even a piece of wood to keep the window open, not that I planned to have it open at night. I usually liked to sleep with fresh air, but I would rather sleep in a locked and bolted room with no chance of entry by anything, human or otherwise.

That done, I turned to have a good look at the room. There was a huge double four poster bed in some sort of darkly varnished wood, and an enormous antique dresser topped with an equally huge mirror. An old rocking chair, also covered in tapestry, sat in one corner, and a heavily upholstered gold brocade armchair sat in the opposite corner. I was pleased to see a pedestal fan near the window. The air was already growing humid, and the gathering black clouds signalled a coming thunderstorm. I usually collected stormwater to use in spells, but there was no way I was going outside, given the circumstances.

I flung open my suitcase and retrieved some comfortable clothes and my make-up bag.

The bathroom was across the hallway from my bedroom. As the aunts' wing was at the front of the house, I would have this bathroom to myself. Still, I wasn't looking forward to having to use it in the night and leaving the safety of my locked bedroom.

I opened the door to the bathroom and, like my bedroom, it was clean. I thought perhaps the aunts had employed a maid to clean it just before I arrived. The whole manor was spic and span. I smiled, grateful that my aunts had taken me in. I knew they genuinely did need help with the business, but I'm sure their motivation was kindness towards me.

The bathroom was small, typical for a home of this age. Of course, when the house had been built, all the bathrooms would have been outside and this would have been added at a later date.

Tiles covered every inch of the room—ceiling excluded, of course. They were off-white, and surprisingly tasteful compared to some other parts of the house I'd seen.

The bath was a heavy claw foot affair, as imposing as it was pretty. I turned on the water and held my hand under it until it ran hot, and then adjusted the temperature. I rummaged through my make-up bag for my cleansing potions. I pulled out a little bottle of dill herbs, and sprinkled some in the bath. Dill was good for removing jinxes. I also selected a little glass vial of *Bluo*, laundry blue. It was a traditional hoodoo method for removing crossed conditions, crossed conditions being otherwise known as curses, hexes, or jinxes. I didn't put too much in the bathwater, because even a tiny bit turned the water bright blue. I also threw in some dried lemongrass. I had grown my own herbs, ones I used for witchcraft, in containers in Sydney, and I wasn't able to bring them on the plane. I had given them away to a neighbour. Here, I would have to start from scratch, but I would have a lot more room to grow my herbs.

It didn't take long for the bath to fill, so I was pleased that the water pressure was good. It wasn't always so in such old houses. I stripped off and threw my clothes just outside the door. It was kind of Aunt Dorothy to do my laundry for me. It was so good to have family again.

I piled up my long hair on top of my head. I just didn't have the energy to wash it. I cleaned my face, a little surprised to see how I looked in the mirror. I tried to reassure myself with the fact that it was probably the harsh light; then again, it was probably the truthful light of day. This bathroom was most likely the brightest room in the house, thanks to the huge windows at the end of the little room. They were frosted, so while no one could see in or out, they nevertheless allowed a great deal of bright daylight to flood the room.

I hopped in the shower and soaped myself, and then quickly rinsed. Soap should never be used in an uncrossing bath, so I had to soap up first. I got out of the shower, careful not to slip on the wet floor, and then lowered myself into the bath.

The temperature was just perfect, and I leaned back with a sigh of delight. The warm water massaged my tense neck muscles, and I wiggled my toes. I remembered that I hadn't unpacked my little plastic jug and placed it next to the bath, but never mind, I was sure the uncrossing would still work. In hoodoo tradition, one should pour bathwater over the head seven times—either that or fully submerge the head, and I wasn't going to do that in the blue water—and then save a cupful of the water to throw out to the east. I wasn't even sure which direction in this house was east, but I would check the compass on my phone later.

I was almost drifting off to sleep when I heard a loud knock on the door. I heard the door creak open and I slid further under the water. "Are you in there, Valkyrie?" Aunt Dorothy's voice asked.

"Yes, Aunt Dorothy."

"I'll just take your clothes and wash them."

"Thank you."

I should have thought to lock the bathroom door. No sooner than I thought that, I heard the door creak open again. "You know, Valkyrie, with what just happened today, you should've locked the bathroom door."

"Thanks, Aunt Dorothy. I'll lock doors from now on."

I lay in the bath so long that it turned cold, and I had to keep topping it up with hot water. I loved baths, but my tiny little apartment had an equally cramped shower, no room for a bath. In fact, there had been no room for anything in that apartment.

Lying in the bath for some time, a sense of inertia set in. I finally willed myself to get out of the bath, despite not having the energy to do so.

I hauled my tired body out of the bath and towelled myself dry, but couldn't find my clothes. I thought I'd put them on the chair next to the door. I poked my head around the door, but there was no sign of my clothes. I groaned. Clearly, when Aunt Dorothy stuck her head in the bathroom, she had taken my clean clothes as well as my dirty ones. No matter. I shut the door and finished drying myself.

I draped the towel around myself and crossed the hallway. I wrapped my hand around the brass door knob and pushed. Nothing happened. It was locked. Why on earth was my bedroom door locked? I tried it a few times, and then with both hands, shook the door knob so hard that my towel almost fell off.

Surely Aunt Dorothy wouldn't have locked my bedroom door when I was in the bathroom? Perhaps it had just jammed. I put my shoulder against it and pushed hard, but it didn't so much as creak.

"Aunt Dorothy?" I called out. There was no response. There was nothing else for it—I would have to go in search of my aunts and the key to my room. I only hoped that the detectives didn't choose this moment to come back to question any of us.

CHAPTER 5

As I made my way downstairs, I somehow got lost. It wasn't too hard to do in Mugwort Manor; it was a veritable labyrinth.

I took a turn left instead of right, and ended up in an eerie corridor I remembered from my childhood. The aunts had always warned me sternly not to go in that wing of the house. They had called it the Forbidden Corridor.

No small wonder; it was straight out of a cheesy horror movie. It was long, and so dark towards the back that I couldn't even see where it ended. The floor was covered in a thin red carpet that barely covered the creaking floorboards beneath, and the walls were set with the same heavy wooden panels as in most other rooms. A strange smell hung in the air, like eucalyptus leaves and the red dust of the Outback, mixed with something pungent, like a wild animal.

My bare feet trembled on the faded Axminster carpet. Was that a vibration I felt? I put my hand on the panelled wall and yes, it did appear to be vibrating a little. I walked around a bend in the hallway and came face-to-face with a door I had always feared.

How had I forgotten? It all came flooding back to me. There was something about that room that held fear for me, something I couldn't quite remember. Many times over the years I had tried to remember, or rather, had thought I should remember but wondered if I really wanted to do so. I suspected that, as a young child, I had seen something in that room that had terrified me.

As I turned hastily to walk away, I saw a pulsating red light emanating from the crack under the door. I stood there, frozen to the spot, my breath caught in my throat.

Part of me wanted to turn and run, but part of me wanted to know what was going on. I crept along the hallway to the room and gingerly reached out my hand for the door knob. I touched the door knob, and when nothing happened, I turned it.

That door, too, was locked. I put my ear to the door and heard Aunt Agnes's voice. It was striking, as if she was commanding someone.

I turned and walked away as fast and as silently as I could. It seemed as if every floorboard creaked. My breathing was laboured as raw fear coursed through me.

When I was safely around the corner, I heaved a sigh of relief.

What was going on in that room? Perhaps it was simply the aunts' altar room. They had said they were witches, and they wouldn't want anyone stumbling across their magical works. That was what I wanted to believe, but I had the niggling feeling that it was something more than that.

My towel was threatening to fall off, so I tucked it back in and made my way to the main staircase.

I went to the laundry first, but there was no sign of anyone, nor was there anyone in the kitchen. The washing machine was whirring away. "Aunt Dorothy," I called loudly.

Perhaps she was having a cup of tea in the living room. I hadn't heard anyone else in the upstairs room with Aunt Agnes. I stuck my head in the living room and called out again. I was beginning to become a little frustrated. I was wearing only a towel, and I was locked out of my room.

I did not know where to look next, but the ringing of the doorbell decided for me. "Aunt Dorothy?" I called out. No one responded, so I figured it had to be her. She was deaf, after all, and any other person would have replied. I hurried to the front door and flung it open. As I did so, my towel caught on a sharp point of the old brass door handle. My towel slipped off me and fell to the ground. I snatched it up and wrapped it back around me, but too late. I looked up into the horrified face of the visitor.

It was Lucas O'Callaghan.

CHAPTER 6

I could have died. I really did want the ground to open up and swallow me.

"I need to speak to your aunts," he said in a clipped tone. "It simply won't work, Miss Jasper. Flashing your wares has no effect on me, of that I can assure you."

I was so filled with rage and embarrassment that I was struck speechless for a moment. He pushed past me and walked straight into the house, uninvited.

"How dare you!" I called out to his retreating back. "I'll have you know I was just in the bath and Aunt Dorothy took my clothes and I was down here looking for her and I called out and you didn't answer, so of course I thought you were Aunt Dorothy!" I was so furious that I spoke too quickly, my words tumbling one over the other.

He turned around, confusion over his face. Okay, it wasn't the best explanation, but I had just flashed my naked self at a stranger, a rude stranger who for some reason known only to himself thought I was after his body.

Aunt Dorothy appeared in the room, looking as shocked as I felt. "What's going on?" she asked, looking me up and down.

"Aunt Dorothy, did you take my clothes? My clean clothes that were on the chair inside the bathroom door when I was in the bath?"

"Oh, were they your clean clothes? I thought they were your dirty clothes. I'm so sorry, dear. Is that why you're wearing a towel?"

I took a deep breath to try to calm myself. "The reason I am wearing a towel," I said slowly and carefully, enunciating each word precisely, "is that my bedroom door was locked. Did you lock my bedroom door?"

Aunt Dorothy walked over to me. "Yes, Valkyrie. You said you wanted your door locked."

I took another long deep breath and let it out

slowly. "Not when I was on the other side of the door, Aunt Dorothy. How did you expect I would get back into my bedroom to get my clothes? And now your guest has accused me of wearing a towel to attract him, or some such thing." I shot him my best glare. This time, I did expect him to apologise.

"I didn't think you were *wearing* a towel to attract me," he said.

"But you said…"

He interrupted me. "I thought you *removed* the towel to attract me."

Heat slowly rose from my toes until it covered my face. My whole body burned with anger. I wanted to say something, but I couldn't think of anything sufficiently censored. I was aware of my mouth opening and shutting, and I became even angrier as I couldn't think of anything suitable to say. Finally, I said through clenched teeth, "My towel got caught in the old brass door knob. If you go and have a look at it, I'm sure you'll see threads of the towel in it. And I don't find you the slightest bit attractive. Sure, you're okay to look at, but your personality leaves a lot to be desired. In fact, I'd call you a pig, but I like pigs—they're nicer than people." I thought that might be going too far given that he was a guest, but then again he had insulted me. I turned to Dorothy. "Aunt Dorothy, may I have my bedroom key?"

"Certainly." She pulled it out of her pocket and handed it to me. I walked up the staircase in my towel with as much dignity as I could muster. I was halfway to the top when the hairs on the back of my neck stood up. I swung around, and Lucas O'Callaghan was staring at me. He whipped his head away as soon as I caught him looking at me. Various emotions coursed through me. I was mortified; I was embarrassed; I was furious.

I dressed hurriedly and did not put on any make-up, in case the irritating Lucas O'Callaghan was still there and thought I had put on make-up specifically to seduce him. That man sure had problems, thinking women were throwing themselves at him. The nerve of him! Talk about conceited.

This time when I went downstairs, I found all the aunts together in the living room. They were staring at their knitting, their knitting needles clacking away ninety to the dozen. Mercifully, there was no sign of O'Callaghan. "Has that man gone?" I asked them.

"Yes," Agnes said.

"What did he want?"

"He came to ask us to stay inside and keep our doors and windows locked."

I frowned. "That was it? But the police already said that. Surely there was more to it?"

Aunt Maude set her knitting down. "He made a long speech to the effect that he'd had a look around outside and thinks we're in danger. He suggested we go and stay with relatives."

I snorted rudely. "That's exactly what the police said. Is he some sort of undercover police officer or something? Or a private detective?" I was puzzled.

"I think he's just an interfering busybody," Maude said. "He thinks we're helpless females."

I thought they were helpless females, too, but I wasn't about to say so. "I think it's very strange for him to come here and say that. If he has any new information, he should go to the police."

The aunts muttered amongst themselves for a moment. Agnes was the first to speak. "He's just an annoying man trying to throw his weight around. Pay him no mind."

I wondered if they were keeping something from me. "Is that all he said?"

The three of them nodded. I bit my lip, but I

did sense that they were telling the truth about that. "What are we going to do?"

"Do?" Aunt Agnes echoed. "We're going to go to the police station and give our witness statements, and then I'm going to prepare dinner. While I'm doing that, maybe you could look at our website and see if it needs tweaking in any way."

"I know you mentioned you had a website," I said, "but I wasn't able to find it, and you weren't able to email me the website address. How do people book?"

"By calling us, of course. There's the telephone on the reception desk. How else would they book?" Agnes looked at me as if I had taken leave of my senses.

I thought I would tackle the whole question of the website later. Clearly, it was going to be a somewhat serious task. "When are we going to give our statements?"

"As soon as you're ready, dear," Dorothy said.

"Okay, just give me a moment to get dressed." I hurried back to my bedroom and put on some better clothes, brushed my hair, and this time applied make-up.

Aunt Agnes drove us to the police station. She had a tiny blue Mazda. I was sitting in the back seat with the ample figure of Aunt Maude. That, coupled with the fact that Aunt Agnes drove like a racing car driver, made the journey somewhat uncomfortable. The road dropped away sharply at some parts. Sure, this was on the coast, but it was headland country, so it rose and fell. I had spent the entire, mercifully short, journey with my eyes firmly shut and clutching my seatbelt with both hands.

As soon as we arrived at the police station, I looked around for O'Callaghan and was relieved that there was no sign of him. Sergeant Carteron was at the front desk, and he smiled broadly when he saw me. "Well hello, Miss Jasper," he said, ignoring the aunts. "I'll just see if the detectives are ready to take your statement now."

I was first in, and it was over more quickly than I thought, nothing like I had seen on TV. I supposed that's because I wasn't a suspect. I figured the detectives had checked with the cab driver and found I had truly arrived in town just prior to the man's murder, and it would also help that I had been standing with the aunts and Mr O'Callaghan when the body fell through the roof. That meant none of us could be the culprit, although there was always the possibility that one of us was in it with someone else, an accomplice.

I shook myself. That had actually not occurred to me before. What if Mr O'Callaghan had an accomplice? Being downstairs in the lobby when the man fell through the roof would have given him an alibi.

When I returned to the waiting room, Aunt Dorothy was on the edge of her seat. "Agnes is giving her statement now," she called across the room, seemingly uncaring that every pair of eyes swivelled to her, "and the police found out who the victim was. That nice sergeant just told us."

I waited, but she didn't volunteer the information. "Who was it?" I asked her.

"It was the wine scientist at the winery," she said. "He worked for Henry Ichor."

"Henry Ichor, the same Henry Ichor who died overseas recently and left his winery to Mr O'Callaghan?"

Both of them nodded solemnly. "The one and the same," Aunt Maude said.

I tapped my chin. The surname sounded familiar. "Henry Ichor died overseas, and now his wine scientist has been murdered. Do you find that a bit suspicious?"

They looked at each other, and it was obvious to me they were wondering how much they should tell me. That meant that they knew something, and I said so. "Please don't keep anything from me. I can tell that you both know something."

"Nonsense, dear," Aunt Maude said. "If we did, we'd tell you."

We stared each other down, but she didn't blink or look away. Finally, I sighed. "Okay, then. I've been thinking it over, and I'm wondering if Lucas O'Callaghan had something to do with it."

Maude's pencilled eyebrows shot skyward. "How could he? He was with us when it all happened."

"Exactly!" I said triumphantly. "That gave him an alibi, while his accomplice was up on the roof murdering that poor man."

Dorothy and Maude exchanged glances once more. "I know you find him irritating, Valkyrie," Dorothy said in a soothing tone, "but he didn't murder that man."

"But you don't know that," I said.

"Agnes thinks he might be useful to us," Maude said.

I was perplexed. "How? How could he possibly be useful to us? Do you mean giving you a discount on the wine?" Before they could answer, I pushed on. "It's quite suspicious, if you ask me. First of all, that Henry guy is killed overseas, and then Lucas O'Callaghan inherits everything. Then the wine scientist was murdered, right when Lucas was at your house. That can't be a coincidence. Maybe the wine scientist knew that Lucas killed Henry."

"Mr O'Callaghan didn't kill anyone," Agnes said.

I started, because I hadn't seen her come into the room, so lost had I been in thought. "Dorothy, it's your turn to go in now," she continued.

Agnes took a seat next to me. "I'm not fond of men, but I do think that Mr O'Callaghan can be useful to us."

"Yes, Aunt Dorothy said you'd said that. Useful in what way?"

Her eyes flickered, and then she said, "Time will tell. Anyway, I invited him for dinner tonight."

My heart sank.

"You know, I had never met Talos Sparkes," Aunt Agnes said. "Still, customers wouldn't normally meet the scientific staff."

I sat upright. "Was that his name? Talos?"

Aunt Agnes's brow creased. "Why yes. Did you know him?"

I shook my head. "I've just remembered where I'd heard the name Ichor before. Now I see why

Henry Ichor named it Ambrosia Winery. I wonder if he was related to Talos? That's surely too much of a coincidence."

Agnes and Maude exchanged glances. "I'm at a loss, Valkyrie," Agnes said. "What on earth are you talking about?"

"Ambrosia, of course!" I said triumphantly. Looking at their blank expressions, I pushed on. "Ambrosia was the food of the mythical Greek gods. You know, the legendary food that made them immortal. That's why Henry Ichor called his winery *Ambrosia*."

"I'm still at a loss," Agnes said. "I thought ichor was a horrible discharge from a wound."

I shook my head. "In mythology, ichor was the blood of the Greek gods, or immortals in general. It was said to contain ambrosia. Only immortals consumed ambrosia."

"Oh that makes sense, dear," Aunt Maude said, although her expression said otherwise.

"And Talos—that name can't be a coincidence," I said. "In mythology, he had a single vein filled with ichor."

Aunt Agnes waved her hand. "I think Henry Ichor was Greek," she said. "That explains it. He probably employed a Greek wine scientist."

I shook my head. "I'm sure they were related. Perhaps Talos's mother was an Ichor."

"And to think some people said your degree in Classical Literature was useless, Valkyrie," Aunt Maude said, shooting a look at Agnes.

CHAPTER 7

I sat in my aunts' dimly lit office, tapping away at their ancient desktop computer. Thank goodness their internet was fast. Thank goodness they had internet at all! My laptop was still packed, and I wondered whether I should go fetch it. Still, this computer had their passwords stored, and I hoped like hell their passwords were written down somewhere.

Their website simply referred to Mugwort Manor, and did not allude to the fact that they were a Bed and Breakfast establishment. The banner up the top showed the lighthouse, but the lighthouse could not be seen from the property.

As I already knew, there was nowhere to book on the website, and that was something I would have to address in a hurry. I was surprised that anyone had ever discovered the website, but discovered it they had, as demonstrated by the huge amount of reviews, none of them favourable.

The first review had the word 'avoid' in capitals three times in a row: AVOID AVOID AVOID. The second review was entitled, *A Journey to Hell*.

I spent several minutes reading the reviews, cringing as I did so. At least every review admitted that the rooms were clean. Most complained about the eccentricity of the aunts, giving lengthy, and I hoped, exaggerated examples, and most complained that the lighthouse was depicted on the website, but they had to walk for five minutes to see it in person.

Several complained that there was no actual breakfast served, but rather baskets of bread, breakfast cereals, coffee, tea, milk, sugar, cookies, and condiments left for them to prepare their own breakfasts. Several also mentioned that they were not told until after their arrival that breakfast would not be served. More than one reviewer said they had brought up this fact to the aunts, but that they had simply responded that they didn't do breakfast any more.

I rubbed my temples furiously and then

wondered where I had left my Advil. I stood up and stretched, and then made yet another attempt to pull the massive curtains aside. These were heavy burgundy velvet, and when I moved them, I was surprised that no dust billowed out. Still, not one review said that the place was dirty.

I had no idea where to make a start in improving the business itself, other than to do a decent website. The other pressing matter was to change the themed cottages. I didn't know how far I would get with that, given that my aunts were attached to and delighted with the themes. And then there were the finances to address—I shuddered when I thought of going through the accounts.

I sat down and turned my attention back to the website. It was clearly a free one, and displayed copious advertising matter, most of it appearing as pop-ups. To the left of the screen was a big square announcing the day's weather and date, and then some allegedly newsworthy items from the district. Some of the photos had not loaded and just appeared as squares on the left-hand side of the page and across the bottom.

Mercifully, the address was there, as was the aunts' telephone number. The bottom of the website was filled with photographs of the area, or so I assumed, given that only the top five had managed to load so far.

I put my head in my hands and groaned. This was an absolute nightmare. I had not been the slightest bit optimistic about what I would find, but this far surpassed my dismal expectations—in a bad way. It was a sad state of affairs, to be sure, and then there was the added problem of a possible murderer about to kill us all in our beds. And as if that wasn't enough, there was Lucas O'Callaghan who was bizarrely convinced that every woman wanted him.

I stood up and stretched once more, thinking I should go and get ready for dinner. I didn't want to dress up too much, as I knew what that awful Lucas would think. I giggled as I fancied I should black out my two front teeth just to irritate him.

I went to my bedroom, happy that it was unlocked—though I intended to take my keys everywhere with me for the foreseeable future to be on the safe side—and changed into a long beach skirt and a brief tank top. I decided not to wear any make-up, but after I cleansed my face, I slathered on some tinted sunscreen. It was oil-based and gave me a glow. I wasn't going to bother with mascara or lip gloss. I'd get a tan soon enough. I tanned easily, but had not spent much of my time in Sydney outdoors. Come to think of it, I had planned to walk along the beach this evening. Well, that wasn't going to happen. I was instead going to have to spend the evening in the company of the dreadful Lucas O'Callaghan.

I walked down to the dining room, but no one was there. I could hear the aunts chattering away in the kitchen. I crossed to the curtains and drew them open. I didn't think they had been opened in years, because they were quite resistant to being moved. I decided not to open the sash windows to let in some fresh air, partly because I knew the aunts would only shut them at once, and also because I didn't know if the murderer was in the vicinity.

The aunts had laid the table beautifully, with a heavy lace tablecloth that looked antique, and fine antique china in a pretty pattern of yellow buttercups. I peeked over the top of the heavy tapestry fire screen to see logs in the fireplace, I supposed simply for decoration as it was the middle of summer. Three yellowing candles sat in each of the two square heavy brass sconces either side of the ornate fireplace, which was white marble with a pair of female marble figures flanking the grate.

A large porcelain vase of fresh flowers sat on a side table, and scented candles sat at intervals down the centre of the dining table. They radiated a strong scent of sweet orange blossom, which all but overpowered the lingering scent of mould that hung unmistakably in the stale air.

I looked down at the ancient antique Persian carpet under my sandaled feet. It had seen better days, as had the rest of the house. Paint was peeling off the walls in several places, creating a kind of eerie silhouette in the dim light. The heavy plaster ceiling was supporting several crystal chandeliers that managed to glimmer beautifully despite the relative darkness.

Several sash windows adorned the walls, each set with solid colour stained glass panels. There were several colours, but they managed to come together in a surprisingly tasteful way, each colour and window complementing the next. It was a nice break from the dreariness of the room.

The chandelier above me tinkled. I spun around. There could be no breeze; the windows were shut. Perhaps it had been a draft down the chimney. There was that fluttering feeling in my stomach again, my right eye twitched, and then the doorbell chimed.

This time, I had no intention of answering it. Let the aunts usher in the insufferable man.

Aunt Agnes and Aunt Maude soon appeared with said insufferable man, along with three other people I hadn't met, or had even known existed.

"Valkyrie, I'd like you and Mr O'Callaghan to meet our other guests, Paul and Linda Williams, and Marius Jones."

Linda Williams walked to me slowly and shook my hand. As I was trying to extract it, I looked over and saw that her husband was doing the same to Lucas. Marius Jones stood off in the background, looking sullen. I judged him to be about thirty years of age, and he was muscle bound. My first thought was that he would be able to drag the body onto the roof, if anyone could.

"I didn't know you had other guests, Aunt Agnes," I said. "I thought your only guest was Mr O'Callaghan." As soon as I said it, I remembered that one of the police officers had mentioned guests in passing.

Aunt Agnes did not look the least put out. "Oh, we haven't had time to tell you, what with everything going on. The three other guests are here for the week, so I thought we should have

them all to dinner, to make up for, well you know..."
Her voice trailed away.

I didn't know how any dinner, no matter how sumptuous, would make up for the fact that a murder had been committed where one was staying.

Aunt Maude bustled around, showing everyone to their seats. To my dismay, I was seated opposite Lucas. I regretted not having the presence of mind to discuss the seating arrangements with my aunts first. I looked around wildly for the vase of flowers I had spotted earlier, wondering if I should place it directly between us.

"Mr O'Callaghan has brought us several bottles of his marvellous wine," Agnes announced to a murmur of approval from all gathered. "Would everyone like some wine?" She whisked the bottle past everyone's eyes. No one declined, not even the grumpy muscular guy. Agnes duly filled our glasses. There was still no expression on Lucas's face.

"I'm so sorry for your loss," Dorothy said to him.

He looked up from his wine glass, startled.

"I mean the victim, of course. The police told us that he was the wine scientist working for your company, the one you just inherited."

"Yes. I had never met him," Lucas said.

"It's still a terrible thing that happened to him, whether you'd met him or not," Agnes pointed out waspishly.

The mask was back. "Quite so."

"Will he be hard to replace? Wine scientists can't be common."

"Yes, he will be very hard to replace," Lucas said in a heartfelt manner. It was the first overt emotion I had heard from him. "He was in fact a distant cousin, but he'd been out of the country for years."

"Aha!" I said.

"Excuse me?"

I didn't think the guests wanted to be subjected to a lesson in Greek mythology, so I said, "I'm sorry about your cousin."

Everyone else murmured their sympathies.

I tried to change the subject from the gloom and doom that had descended over the table. "I'm Pepper Jasper," I said to the three guests. "I'll be staying here for some time to help my aunts."

Linda Williams fixed her gaze on me. I don't think she liked what she saw. She was short, slender, and pale, and while her features were pleasant, her expression was not. There was something about her that I couldn't quite put my finger on, neither overtly predatory nor passive aggressive, but perhaps somewhere in between. After staring at me for a moment, she finally spoke. "So you'll be helping your aunts? You're not working?"

I didn't know if the implication was that I was sponging off my aunts, but I was determined not to take offence. "I'll be working here," I said. "I'm going to help my aunts with this business."

Her husband spoke. "What are your qualifications?" His manner was as unpleasant as his wife's, if not more so.

I hesitated. "Um, I have an Arts degree," I said somewhat defensively, "majoring in Classical Literature, and I've watched every season of *The Hotel Inspector*. Every episode."

A strange sound came from Lucas's throat. I glared at him, and then turned my attention to the unpleasant couple. "What do you do, Mr Williams?" He wasn't the only one who could play twenty questions.

"I'm a taxidermist," he announced proudly.

"Oh." I could think of nothing else to say. "And you, Mrs Williams?"

"I support my husband," she said primly.

"Um, that's nice," I muttered after an interval.

Aunt Dorothy leaned forward. "A taxi driver, did you say, Mr Williams?"

He straightened in his chair. "No, a taxidermist. I stuff animals."

No one responded. A heavy silence descended over the table, a silence so thick I could almost reach out and touch it. I fervently hoped someone else would make conversation.

Thankfully, Aunt Agnes did. "What is your line of work, Mr. Jones?"

I expected he would simply grunt, so I was surprised when he said more than five words. "I'm a body builder. My anger management therapist sent me here to the sea, to get away from the whole bodybuilding scene. I mean, it's a good scene, don't get me wrong, but I got hooked on steroids. I got so hooked on them that I started dealing in them." He paused to draw breath, and tapped one of his bulging biceps. "This isn't natural, trust me. Most of my muscle gain is from steroids."

"But you've given them up now?" I asked, curious in spite of myself, and then regretted speaking when I saw Lucas's eyes on me. I supposed he thought I would throw myself at Marius.

"Have you served time in prison?" Linda asked, her lips tightly pursed.

Marius turned to look at her, his face at once bright red. "No," he said angrily. "It's all in my past. I've reformed." I noticed he was clenching and unclenching his fists.

I sized him up. He had gone from calm and polite to angry in an instant. He was bulked up on steroids and was the most likely person to have the ability to carry a man onto the roof. Plus he had anger management issues. I made a mental note to go outside and look for a way onto the roof. I would do that, in daylight, the following morning.

Aunt Dorothy stood up. "I'll get the iced avocado soup."

I stood up, too. "I'll help you." I was in the process of pushing back my chair when Aunt Maude spoke up.

"No, you stay here and chat with our guests. I'll help her."

At that moment, I made the inopportune decision to glance at Lucas. After all, he was sitting directly in front of me. Unfortunately for me, he caught my eye. I looked away immediately, and then realised that had only made things worse. It would no doubt reinforce his opinion that I was interested in him.

An uncomfortable silence once more descended

over the table, broken only when the black cat from earlier that day walked into the room. Had it been earlier that day? It seemed like a lifetime ago. So much had happened in this one day. If only I could go back in time and start again. It would involve no murders, no supercilious men.

"That cat shouldn't be allowed in the dining room," Paul shrieked loudly. "It's unhygienic. I've a good mind to report this to the Health Inspector."

"I will remind you that this is a private dining room, and nothing to do with my aunts' business itself," I said in the most even tone I could muster. "My aunts invited you to dinner out of the goodness of their hearts, not as anything to do with the business."

Paul did not appear to know how to respond. He muttered to himself and waved his napkin around with a flourish.

"I like cats," Marius said. "What's her name?"

I spoke quickly, before Agnes had a chance. "We don't know. She just visits here. She doesn't live in the manor." I was careful not to say my aunts didn't own her, because that could set off Aunt Agnes into a flurry of eccentric speech.

"She arrived here some time ago, quite malnourished," Aunt Dorothy said. "We thought she was a stray. We feed her, but we don't know where she lives, because she comes and goes."

"Did you take her to a vet to see if she's microchipped?" I asked them.

The aunts looked confused. "What's that?" Aunt Dorothy asked me.

"You know, a microchip." I looked at their blank faces, so I continued. "By law, every cat in Australia must have a microchip, and the owner's details are registered with the local council. If pets get lost, vets can scan them and reunite them with their owners."

"Oh, is that what it was?" Dorothy asked me. "We took her to the vet and she did wave a little machine over her. We left details with the local pound, too, but no one ever contacted us to say anyone had turned up for her."

"I'll take the cat out of the room and turn on the TV for her," Agnes announced. She left the room, cradling the cat in her arms. Paul glowered at me from under his eyebrows and Linda pouted. I noticed Marius was speaking, so I forced myself to pay attention to his words. "And so, does anyone know if the police have got any clues as to the murderer?" he said.

"I told you we should go and book somewhere else," Linda said in a stage whisper to her husband.

"And I told you that we've already paid in advance," he said tersely.

"I'm sure they'll give us a refund. After all, there's been a murder."

"I'm the new business manager, and I'm sorry, but our policy is that we cannot give refunds under any circumstances. Of course, you're welcome to go and stay elsewhere," I said with rather more enjoyment than I should have, "but a refund is out of the question."

Linda pursed her lips and said nothing.

"Do the police know why he was on the roof?" Marius asked.

I shrugged. "If they do, they haven't told us."

Marius leaned across the table and looked at Lucas, who had been sipping his wine. "They say your cousin was a wine scientist who worked for your uncle. Why would a wine scientist be on the roof of this building?"

"Why would a wine scientist be on the roof of *any* building?" I said with a shrug.

"I had never met my cousin," Lucas said patiently. "There's obviously a logical explanation. I've only just taken over my uncle's business and I don't know any of the staff. I don't know why he was on the roof."

As the others chatted, I thought it through. It wasn't as if the victim was a naturalist studying starlings or possums or any other species that hung about in a roof. No, there was no logical explanation. The more I thought about it, the more it seemed clear to me that the wine scientist was murdered in that manner either to provide Lucas O'Callaghan with an alibi or to threaten him. If it were the latter, then I figured that the man had been murdered, carried to the roof of the house, and thrown through the skylight right in front of Lucas O'Callaghan solely as a warning. It was strange that two relatives had died in a short space of time, at least one of them murdered, and his body thrown at the feet of his cousin.

Was someone upset that Lucas had inherited the winery? Was this tied up with Henry Ichor's death? I had no idea, but I had confidence that the detectives would sort it out. One thing was clear: this murder had everything to do with Lucas O'Callaghan.

That night, I lay in my bed. I had pulled the heavy dresser across the door after I locked it, and I had made sure the window was firmly bolted. I had checked under the bed and in the wardrobe. I had taken the longest knife I could find from the kitchen and put it under my pillow, and I was clutching my phone. Still, I had only taken a quick glance at the victim's injuries, and it didn't look as though he had any warning or any success in fighting off his attacker.

I hoped that when I woke up the following morning, there would be no more incidents. Even if there were, I figured that my aunts and I should be safe. It all seemed to focus on Lucas. A warm glow bubbled away in the pit of my stomach when I thought of him, much to my annoyance. The man was irritating, but still, I felt an almost chemical attraction towards him. There was just something about him. I tossed and turned all night, and only part of that could be attributed to my wonder as to what could be lurking outside.

CHAPTER 8

$\mathcal{I}$ hadn't been able to sleep well at all. Somehow, in the middle of the night, I had opened the curtains so I would see anyone trying to climb in. It was a brightly waxing moon, so I figured I would see an intruder before they would see me. It had seemed like a good idea at the time.

This time, I was jolted awake, struggling for breath. I'd had a nightmare, but I couldn't quite remember what it was about. The fear from my nightmare clung to me, but the light flooding through the windows gave me some respite.

I was still hanging onto my phone, so I looked at the screen. It was only six. I debated going back to sleep for an hour, but as I was unusually alert for this time of day, I decided I might as well get up and have some coffee. I pushed the large chest out of the way of my bedroom door, and peeped into the corridor. There was not a soul in sight. I hurried into the bathroom, and locked the door behind me. I had a quick shower, brushed my hair, and slapped on some moisturiser. It was then I remembered that I had left my fresh clothes in my bedroom. I wasn't used to living in such a large house. In my tiny apartment, the bathroom was accessed through my bedroom. I unlocked the bathroom door, crossed the hallway, unlocked my bedroom door and let myself in. This was no way to live—I hoped the police would catch the murderer soon.

I tiptoed downstairs, careful not to wake up my aunts. In the kitchen, I was surprised to see they had an espresso machine. I was delighted, and even more delighted when I found the coffee capsules. I turned on the machine to warm, and then decided to go outside and see how anyone could get up on the roof. I had been burning with curiosity about that matter all night. I walked out the kitchen door which was at the back of the house and walked sufficiently far into the garden so I could see the whole back wall at once.

I shook my head. Only Spiderman would be

able to get up that. My gaze fell on the large, spreading Alder tree at the side of the house. I walked over to it. I had climbed this tree as a child. I hadn't climbed too far, but it was the sort of tree that children like to climb. Still, there was no way anyone could climb it all the way to the roof of the building. Then I had a thought. If someone had a long ladder, perhaps they would be able to climb it, with the man's body over their back, and hold onto the branches of the tree for support. It seemed a fanciful idea, but someone had managed to get that man onto the roof somehow.

I climbed up the tree as best I could, but didn't get too far, as I expected. I sat in a fork of the branches for a while, wondering what to do next, when I remembered the old garden shed. It was just to my left, made of corrugated iron on a brick base. And was that an old ladder I could see next to it?

I gingerly let myself down from the tree, landed a little too heavily, and then walked briskly over to the garden shed. The old ladder was on the ground, running the length of the small shed. I picked it up, and half carried, half dragged it to the wall of the house.

I intended to climb up, not all the way to the

top, but a short distance to see if the branches would lend support to someone carrying a body.

The ladder was wooden, and heavy, and it was all I could do to prop it up against the wall of the building. It seemed unlikely to me that the murderer had used this ladder, but it would do for the purposes of my experiment. Spiky green moss oozed from its pores that reached deep below its surface. I wondered if it would even hold my weight.

After a struggle, I leaned the ladder against the wall of the building, directly under the spreading Alder tree. I tested one rung, the lowest. It held my weight. I gripped the edges of the ladder and bounced up and down a little. Success. It didn't so much as creak. I tried the next rung, and then the next. I had positioned the ladder evenly on the damp ground, and it didn't quiver in the slightest.

I was past the fork in the tree now, and I carefully looked above me. I could see another fork a little further up the tree. I wondered if the murderer had climbed up the ladder and then crossed to the tree and continued his climb from there. Thick leaves hung directly above me, so I thought I should try just one more rung. That was my undoing.

It only held my weight for a moment and then gave way.

I screamed as I fell backwards. My descent seemed to happen in slow motion, giving me time to wonder how many bones I would break when I hit the ground.

Instead of the ground, I fell backwards into someone's arms. The momentum flipped me over; I landed directly on top of him. To my abject horror, I found myself lying directly on top of Lucas O'Callaghan, my legs straddling his.

We were so close that I could feel his warm breath on my cheek. He smelled divine, of clove, cinnamon, and rosemary. My hands were resting on his chest, and his arms were around me.

When I had fallen from this very tree as a child, I had stayed still on the ground, checking movement in each limb, one by one, to make sure I wasn't hurt. This time, I scrambled to my feet as fast as I could.

Lucas likewise stood up. I was relieved he seemed unharmed, but I knew what he would think, that I had thrown myself at him—literally. He opened his mouth to speak, but I forestalled him. "I didn't know you were there!" It came out as an accusation.

"Are you all right?" he asked, concern evident in his voice.

"I'm sorry I fell on you, really I am, but don't you dare suggest I did it deliberately!" My voice was shrill, but I didn't care. "Look up there," I continued, pointing to the ladder. "See that broken rung? It gave way and I fell. I wasn't trying to land on you."

"I take it you're not hurt, then?" he said dryly.

"No." I patted my hands over my body. "No, I don't think so. Thanks for catching me." I narrowed my eyes as I said it.

"What were you doing on the ladder? You weren't trying to climb onto the roof, were you?"

"Of course not," I said, irritated. "The ladder isn't that long, obviously. I was wondering how the murderer got Talos Sparkes onto the roof, so I came here to check out the tree, to see how a man could've climbed onto the roof while carrying a body. There's a lower fork in the tree, and then one much higher, so I wondered if someone climbed the ladder to the second fork and then climbed across onto the tree."

I thought Lucas would dismiss my words, but he walked over to the tree, and swung himself onto the lower fork with the grace of a ballet dancer or an acrobat. I was impressed, in spite of myself. He then disappeared from sight, hidden by the leaves, so I walked over to the tree to peer up into the branches.

Soon his voice called down from the tree, "Move aside, in case I fall."

I did as I was asked. Within moments, Lucas dropped beside me. He moved so fast that I didn't see him coming.

"You're right," he said, "for the most part, anyway. I think someone would be able to climb the tree all the way to the roof. There are some broken branches up there, too. I don't think the culprit needed a ladder, after all."

"That makes sense," I said. "I wouldn't have thought the murderer would have had time to get back down the ladder and hide it away somewhere before the police went outside looking for him. So you're quite sure someone could've climbed the tree all the way to the top? I used to be good at climbing trees when I was a kid, and I didn't think I would be able to do it."

Lucas was standing close to me now, so close I could smell his cinnamon soap, and I instinctively took a step backwards. I saw his face register my movement and it was apparent to me that he was considering what that meant. Perhaps he realised I was not going to make advances to him, after all.

"I'm fairly athletic. I'd be able to climb the tree all the way to the roof, but I doubt I'd be able to do it carrying a body."

"Someone managed to do it," I pointed out.

Lucas nodded. "True. It would have to be a very strong man."

"Stronger than you? You look very strong," I said, and then instantly regretted my words. "Don't flatter yourself," I added hastily. "That was a simple statement of fact, not a compliment."

His lips quirked slightly upward. "I see. Yes, I consider myself strong, but the murderer must've been someone stronger."

I bit my lip. "It just seems impossible that someone would be able to do it." I looked up at the ladder again. "Well, I'd better put this ladder away before anyone else wants to climb up it."

I stepped across to the wall and seized the ladder, but Lucas appeared beside me. Once again, I didn't see or hear him move. "Allow me," he said.

I nodded. He lightly brushed against me as he picked up the ladder, sending an electric jolt through my body. He shot a look at me, and I wondered if he'd felt it, too. I shook my head to clear it. I wasn't a morning person, and I needed coffee. That would put everything into perspective.

Still, I could not help but admire the way his muscles rippled under his thin shirt when he easily picked up the ladder as if it were made of foam. I could barely tear my eyes away. I remembered the feel of his hard chest muscles under my hands.

"I got it from there, next to the shed. You can see the marks in the grass."

He placed the ladder where I indicated.

"Thanks for that, and for catching me," I said. "Goodbye." I walked swiftly to the back door of the manor, fully conscious of his eyes on my back. I could feel them burning into me.

CHAPTER 9

I opened the door and walked straight into the kitchen. The aunts were making breakfast and bickering.

"I saw you talking to that man," Agnes said. "What were you doing with the ladder?"

I explained as quickly as I could, but they didn't seem surprised. I bet they had somehow been listening, but I didn't see how that was possible. The coffee machine was well and truly warmed up by now, so I slipped in a high intensity strength capsule and smiled with delight when the coffee poured into my cup, making a delicious golden crema on top of the dark inviting liquid.

There was no point being attracted to Lucas O'Callaghan. For all I knew, he could be an accomplice to the murder, and if he wasn't, he was arrogant and conceited. No, I just had to resist the electric tingles that consumed my body every time he was within my proximity.

"What are you having for breakfast, Valkyrie?" Aunt Maude asked me.

"I don't usually have breakfast," I said. "I usually just have coffee. I'm not a breakfast person. I generally have a snack later in the day when I get hungry."

All three aunts looked shocked. "But you need to eat a big breakfast," Aunt Agnes said. "It's the most important meal of the day."

"Okay then, I suppose I could try some toast." I popped some bread in the toaster.

Soon the four of us were sitting around the large, round wooden table in the middle of the kitchen. It was a large room, even by the manor's standards. A floating island stood separated from a wall covered with cupboards, drawers, and cooking essentials, such as an oven and sink. The table was quite close to the island bench, but not so close as to constrain movement from those of us sitting.

The floor was covered in wide tallow wood floorboards, set off nicely by thick wooden beams on the ceiling. I thought that it was one of the nicest rooms in the house, and would only be nicer with a little more natural light.

I spread some vegemite on my toast and then took a large mouthful. It did taste good. Perhaps I could get used to eating breakfast, after all. It was so kind of my aunts to take me in, so lovely to have a sense of family after the past five years that my parents had been missing.

The shrill sound of the doorbell nearly made me choke on a piece of toast. "We're not expecting anyone, are we?" Aunt Maude asked.

"No, we're not." Agnes pushed her chair away from the table and pulled herself to her feet. I noticed she and Aunt Maude exchanged glances. The tension rose in the room and set my stomach fluttering. My right eye twitched.

I sipped some coffee while I waited for Agnes to return. To my surprise, she returned with Sergeant Carteron. He looked a bit sheepish. "I've just come to ask a few questions," he said.

"But it's not yet eight in the morning," Aunt Dorothy protested. "Isn't it a bit early for interrogations?"

Sergeant Carteron's tone was soothing. "Certainly, I don't intend to interrogate you. No one here's a suspect. I start work at nine, so I wanted to come around first and ask some questions off the record."

"Off the record?" I repeated.

"Yes." He shifted from one foot to the other.

"Would you like some coffee?" I asked him. "Please have a seat."

He thanked me and sat down, but it was only when he did so that I was aware of the tension at the table. My aunts clearly didn't want the sergeant to sit with us, and I didn't know why. The sergeant himself appeared oblivious to the taut atmosphere and thanked me warmly when I handed him a steaming mug of coffee.

"Aren't the detectives the ones investigating this matter?" Agnes asked, fixing him with a steely glare.

"Yes, and that's why I'm here off the record," the sergeant explained. When no one spoke further, he continued. "I know I haven't been in town long, but I'm quite attached to Lighthouse Bay. In fact, I intend to stay here for years. The detectives are from out of town and don't have the same vested interest."

"Are you saying they're not exactly doing their job?" I asked.

"I'm not saying that," the sergeant said with a

wink, "but I would like to do a bit of nosing around on my own, entirely off the record."

"Do the detectives have any new information?" Agnes asked him. "Since you've told us your secret, I thought you could share that information with us."

I had to admire her. That was a veiled threat, if ever I'd heard one. I wondered if the sergeant realised that she was subtly threatening to tell the detectives he was asking questions if he didn't share information with us.

If the sergeant harboured any resentment, he didn't show it. "The detectives are quite stumped, to be honest," he said. "That's why I'm here. If I share some information with you, can I have your word it won't go any further?"

All four of us nodded, but I could see my aunts were still eyeing him warily.

"They think it's tied up with your guest, Lucas O'Callaghan." He smiled as if he had given us a piece of juicy information.

"But that's obvious," I said. "The victim was the wine scientist working for the winery, the winery that Lucas O'Callaghan has just inherited, and the body was thrown at his feet only minutes after he arrived in town. What's more, they were related.

Of course it's not a coincidence, Sergeant Carteron."

The sergeant was still smiling. "Please call me Owen. And my policing instincts are usually fairly good, Valkyrie, if I may call you Valkyrie?"

I shook my head. "Please call me Pepper."

"Pepper. Is there something you're not telling me?" He leaned across the table, and I could feel a shift in the room.

"I'm not deliberately withholding information from you, but something happened just before you arrived. I was going to call the detectives later and tell them."

His eyes glittered with an almost animal alertness, like a dog when offered a treat. "What is it?"

"I was just outside, wondering how anyone managed to get up on the roof, and that's when I realised there was the tall Alder tree. I used to climb the lower limbs as a child when I visited my aunts. There's a fork low in the tree, and there's a fork higher up." I was about to mention that Lucas had climbed the tree, when the butterflies in my stomach started again and my right eye twitched. I interpreted that as a warning not to mention his name—why, I didn't know, but I went with it. "I climbed onto the lower fork and then looked up the tree. I could see broken branches up high. I wouldn't be able to climb up there, but I'm sure anyone who was athletic would be able to climb it. There were quite a few broken tree branches. I'm sure they'd be able to get hair and blood samples from it. I think that was the way the murderer got onto the roof."

The sergeant looked at me with admiration. "You're quite the detective, aren't you?" I didn't know how to respond, but he pushed on. "Still, I caution you to be safe. Just leave the detecting to the detectives."

"But you're taking the detective work into your own hands," Aunt Agnes pointed out.

"I'm a police officer."

We were silent; there was no comeback to that.

The sergeant turned his attention to me. "Pepper, call the detectives and tell them exactly what you told me, but please don't mention I was here."

I agreed.

He set down his coffee cup. "Well, that will be all, ladies. Thanks for the coffee. Pepper, would you walk me out?"

"Sure." I wondered what he wanted to say to

me, and I could see that the aunts did, too. They tried to mask their concern, but I could see through it, as I knew them well. I doubted the sergeant would know anything was amiss.

He didn't say anything on the walk to the door, even when we had to skirt the police tape. I opened the door for him.

He stood in the doorway, and faced me. "Valkyrie, sorry, Pepper, would you have lunch with me today?"

I nodded awkwardly and muttered something unintelligible. I didn't know what to say. I didn't particularly want to have lunch with him, but I couldn't think up an excuse on the spur of the moment. After all, I wasn't used to attractive men asking me out and me having to come up with an answer to refuse them.

"Do you know where the Tall Olives Italian Restaurant is? It's in the main street."

"I'm sure I'll find it easily enough," I said, wondering if it was still too late to come up with a good excuse to refuse.

"Okay then, see you at twelve. My shift ends at twelve, so don't worry if I'm a few minutes late." He shot me one last smile and walked out the door.

I shut the door, locked it, and leaned back

against it. What on earth had I gotten myself into? I hadn't come to Lighthouse Bay to look for a date, far from it. And as attractive and as handsome as the sergeant was, there was just something off about him. There was no chemistry there. Besides, a man had just been murdered only a short distance from where I now stood.

I was still leaning against the door when Aunt Agnes came into the room. "What did he want?" she asked me.

"He asked me to join him for lunch today."

Aunt Maude made to speak, but Agnes shushed her. "And how do you feel about that, Valkyrie?"

I walked over to them. "I don't really want to go, but couldn't think up a suitable excuse on the spot."

"Just keep your wits about you and you'll be okay," Aunt Agnes said.

I thought that a strange thing to say, but before I could ask her what she meant, the three aunts turned and left the room. I shrugged. Perhaps she didn't mean anything by it.

"You made sure to lock the front door, didn't you?" Agnes called out to me over her shoulder.

I answered in the affirmative, but just then the

doorbell rang. The aunts came back to the edge of the room.

I opened the door, to see the two detectives, Banks and Anderson, on the doorstep. "May we come in?" Detective Anderson asked before I had a chance to speak. I opened the door wide by way of answer. "We'll take the police tape down now, and you ladies are free to use the foyer again."

The aunts converged on them. "Valkyrie, tell the detectives what you just found out," Agnes said in a commanding tone.

"I was just about to call you," I said. "I remembered that I used to climb the big tree at the side of the house when I was a child, and it occurred to me that the murderer reached the roof by way of the tree. I went out to the tree this morning and had a look, and I could see another fork higher up the tree. I figured if the murderer was a very agile person, then he would've been able to climb the tree all the way to the roof while carrying a body."

Anderson and Banks looked at each other, and I had the sensation that they already knew. And then again, I supposed they did. The tree surely presented the only possible logical explanation.

Instead of responding, Anderson asked, "Do you have a dog as a pet?"

The black cat walked past and hissed at the detectives. "No, we don't have dogs," Aunt Agnes said. "We're cat people, not dog people."

"Yes, we like dogs," Maude said, "but we're those stereotypical old cat ladies that you see on TV. You know, the ones who are spinsters and are surrounded by cats. We're only surrounded by one cat. Not that one cat can surround anyone, but I'm sure you know what I mean."

I zoned out as she continued to babble away. I thought that a rather strange thing for the detective to say, and it had obviously startled Aunt Agnes, judging by the look she was giving him.

"Have you seen any dogs around here lately?" Anderson asked.

We all shook our heads. "And the guests don't have pets either," Aunt Dorothy added.

"You don't allow pets here?" Banks asked.

Aunt Agnes nodded. "Yes, we do allow pets, because our business consists of self-contained cottages. The cottages all have small fenced yards, and we're a pet friendly establishment. It's just that the current guests don't have pets."

I had a sudden moment of clarity. "You've

already taken samples from the tree, haven't you? And you found dog hair there, so the murderer is someone who owns a pet dog." I said it more as a statement than a question.

Detective Banks's expression did not change, but he crossed his arms over his chest and leaned backward. "I can't comment on that, but I ask you not to make that remark to anyone else."

I nodded. At least it was good to know the detectives were on the job after all, and had already taken samples from the tree. Yet surely wouldn't Sergeant Carteron know that? I supposed not, upon reflection. From the little I knew of detectives, they didn't share their information with the uniformed police unless they had to.

Detective Banks stepped forward. "Nothing happened last night? You didn't hear any noises?"

We all said that we hadn't. I was still stuck on the idea of the pet dog. "Remember I told you that I heard growling in the bushes when I arrived? Perhaps the murderer's pet dog was with him."

Sergeant Anderson's usually impassive face crinkled into a frown. "It seems unlikely the murderer would take a pet with him when he was about to perpetrate a crime," he said.

I at once felt foolish. "Of course." I added, "But

it *is* strange that I heard a loud growl in the bushes only moments before the man was murdered."

Aunt Agnes patted my arm. "Oh well, Valkyrie, the police know what they're doing. I'm sure they'll have that nasty murderer behind bars in no time at all, and then we'll all feel safe at night in our beds. Isn't that right, Detective?"

"We're doing our best," he said gruffly. "Good day, ladies."

I watched the detectives walk down the flagstone pathway. I had the feeling the aunts knew something that they weren't telling me. I considered asking them, but I knew them well enough to know that they wouldn't share information unless they truly wanted to do so. There was no way I'd be able to get anything out of them.

My right eye twitched.

CHAPTER 10

*O*wen snapped his fingers at the waiter as we hovered in the lobby, waiting to be seated. I cringed. Any man who snaps at a waiter is not a man I was all that keen on seeing. I thought I wouldn't actually mind seeing Lucas, what with the dark blue eyes and the stubble and that jacket, the one who likely said, 'Yes, I ride a motorcycle, and yes, I did lots of naughty things in high school and yes, I am my grandmother's favourite, because she's always found my devilish antics charming.'

"Are you okay?" Owen asked, pressing his hand into the small of my back as we walked towards our table. The table was at the back, near a spreading fern.

"Fine," I replied. "Fine." I was lying, of course. What was I doing here? I knew the answer. I was here because I wasn't fast enough to think on my feet, and because I was probably more of a people-pleaser than I wanted to admit. My first instinct had been to refuse, and I should have done so. Still, I was here now, and I would just have to make the most of it, whatever that entailed.

I sat in silence while Owen studied the menu. I usually didn't have an appetite before five in the afternoon, but I made up for it after that. The aunts had not wanted me to have lunch with Owen, and I didn't know why. That only served to reinforce the feeling I had that the aunts were hiding something from me. And then there was the mysterious room. What was that strange sound, and the strange light that came from it?

Still, it was awfully kind of the aunts to offer me a job, and it was lovely to have family around me again. My mind wandered to my parents, and I tried not to think about them. It was too upsetting; not knowing what had happened was torture in itself.

Were the aunts doing something illegal, and was that why they didn't want me to get too close to

Owen? If they were doing something illegal, then they clearly weren't putting the proceeds back into the business. I had spent the last few hours going over the books, and while I wasn't mathematically inclined, even I could see that they were barely breaking even.

Still, there was plenty I could do to improve the business. A decent website with online booking was the first thing I had to do, and then I had to change the decor of the cottages. Not surprisingly, not one person online had praised the themed cottages. Rather, they had made disparaging, even cutting, remarks.

I was sure I would be able to improve the business by attending to the major problems. The cottages did not afford a sea view, but I did not think that would be a problem given that the beach was only a short walk away. The cottages themselves were well presented from the outside, and the grounds were nicely kept. I was optimistic I would be able to improve the occupancy rates. However, Mugwort Manor looked unkempt from the outside, but that was the least of my worries. I pulled out my iPhone and made a list: fix the themes; change the website; enable online booking.

I smiled and looked up at Owen, but he was still staring at the menu. Clearly, he was a man who took his food seriously. I turned my attention to the menu just as I saw the waiter making his way towards us.

The waiter looked at me expectantly, his pen paused over his notepad. "Could I have the Greek salad please, but no onions?" I said.

"We don't have onions in our Greek salad," he said with a superior air.

"Onions make me quite sick, so I always have to check," I said. It was bad enough having food intolerances, without encountering the attitude that intolerances prompted from time to time in some of the hospitality industry.

He turned up his nose and looked at Owen. "I'll have the largest T-bone steak you have, rare, with mushroom sauce, fries, and vegetables." The waiter scrawled for a moment and then handed Owen the wine list.

Owen handed it to me. "Do you see anything you like?"

I handed it back to him. "I'm not a big wine drinker. You choose. Hey, what about the local wine, the one that Lucas O'Callaghan's family makes?"

By the look on his face, anyone would have thought I had suggested a glassful of squashed funnel web spiders.

"Oh, isn't his wine any good?" I hastened to say.

"Oh no, nothing like that," he said. "I'm sure it's excellent wine, but I just prefer this one." He tapped his finger on the wine menu.

"Yes, that will suit me fine," I said. I wondered about his strange reaction. I was sure I hadn't imagined it. I also wondered why he had invited me to lunch. He hadn't flirted with me, even in the most minimal way. He hadn't done so much as say I looked nice.

For the first time since we had met outside the door of the restaurant, Owen turned his attention to me. "So, Pepper, why did you return to Lighthouse Bay?"

"I haven't returned as such," I said, "because I've never lived here. I visited many times as a child, but my parents didn't get on too well with my aunts."

He interrupted me. "Why was that?"

"They never did say specifically, but I guess it was because my aunts are quite eccentric."

The waiter came over and poured wine for

Owen to taste. He did so quickly, and then the waiter poured wine into our glasses. I sipped the wine, and thought it not as good as the wine that Lucas had brought to dinner the previous night, but of course I kept my opinions to myself.

"So where are you from?"

I set down my wine glass. "Sydney. I did my degree in Classical Literature there, and then just a variety of temporary jobs."

"What sort of job would someone get after doing that type of degree?" He downed his glass in one go and then poured himself another.

I laughed. "That's just the point. There really isn't one, but I suppose I should've thought of that before I started the degree."

Owen raised his eyebrows. "You didn't think of a career path before you enrolled?"

I shook my head. His tone appeared to be lecturing, but perhaps I was just overly sensitive.

The food arrived, and Owen tucked into it greedily. The conversation came to a complete halt while we ate. I wasn't particularly hungry, so picked the olives out of my salad to eat them. It didn't take me long, but by the time I did so, Owen had finished his meal. He dabbed at his mouth with his napkin.

"You must've been hungry," I said.

"I haven't eaten for ages," he said. "Well, snacks, but not a decent meal."

I nodded, not knowing what else to say. The waiter appeared and handed us dessert menus. "Excuse me for saying so, sir, but are you Ethan's brother?"

"You know Ethan?"

The waiter nodded. "He's buying the car dealership from my sister-in-law's family. Do you happen to know where he is? He was supposed to sign the papers yesterday."

Owen's face turned red. "No, I never know what my brother's doing from one minute to the next." He took my menu from me and handed both his and mine back to the waiter. "I never have dessert," he said tersely.

"Sorry about that," he added when the waiter left.

I nodded politely. I had been looking forward to dessert. I thought Owen rather overbearing, even rude. I wondered why he had invited me to lunch. Surely it wasn't just to comment on my poor choice of career path.

He did, mercifully, order coffee, and I followed suit.

"How long have your aunts lived at Mugwort Manor?" he asked me.

I shrugged. "The family's lived there for ages. It's the ancestral home," I said. "I only wish the ancestors had kept it in a better state of repair."

"Did your family have much to do with the Ichor family?" He leaned forward and once again his eyes glittered.

"I don't have a clue," I said.

"Is Lucas O'Callaghan a friend of your aunts?"

"No, not at all," I said, starting to think this was more like a police interrogation than a date. "They met him only moments after I met him for the first time—you know, right before the body fell through the roof. I don't think they like him."

I immediately regretted my off-the-cuff remark. "Why would you say that?" he asked, his eyes strangely glittering once more.

"They just don't like men in general. They've never been married, and they're elderly. They always make disparaging remarks about men."

"Like what?"

Yes, definitely an interrogation. "Just that no one needs a man, that type of thing." I crossed my arms over my chest, but just then the coffee arrived.

"Why are you asking me so many questions?" I asked him when the waiter left.

He laughed. "I'm so sorry. I can't seem to stop being a cop. Please forgive me." He smiled at me winningly, only I wasn't won over, because he had refused dessert on my behalf. I certainly hoped he didn't ask me out again, but I had prepared a good reason in advance if he did.

"How do you feel about vampires and werewolves?"

"Excuse me?" I wasn't sure I had heard him properly.

"I just bought a funny spoof documentary on vampires and werewolves," he said. "It was made in New Zealand. I've heard it's good, so I was wondering if you'd like to come over to my place some time and see it."

I bit my lip and tried not to shudder at the thought of going to Owen's house alone. "I don't like that sort of thing. I only like romantic comedies. That would give me nightmares."

A child at a nearby table shrieked. I jumped, but Owen didn't react. "So what do you know about the other guests staying with your aunts?"

"Oh, it's the twenty questions again, is it?" I said, keeping my tone light.

He simply smiled and didn't speak.

I decided to answer. It was better than talking about watching a movie at his house. "As far as I know, they haven't stayed at Mugwort Manor before, and my aunts haven't ever met them. Do you know, the detectives came over earlier and said they had already taken material from the roof and the tree, and they found dog hair." I was trying to turn the conversation away from possible future dates.

"Oh, really?" I could see he was doing his best to look surprised, but he would never win an Oscar.

"Yes, really." I wondered why he hadn't told me that he already knew about the dog hair. "That means that the murderer owns a dog, or has had close contact with a dog."

"It seems so." He spun his coffee cup around and looked into it for a moment. "Do your aunts have a pet dog?"

"No, they're cat ladies. I've never known them to have a pet dog, but there's always been at least one cat hanging around them. And before you ask, it's a pet friendly establishment, but none of the guests have any pets with them at the moment. Do you think that's strange?"

He seemed taken aback by my question. "What's strange?"

"That no one at the Bed and Breakfast has a pet dog, and my aunts don't have a pet dog, but there was dog hair on the roof. Either that, or in the tree."

He shook his head. "No, I don't find that strange at all. It just means that it's unlikely one of the guests staying with your aunts is the murderer."

"But you do think the murder's connected with Lucas O'Callaghan, don't you?"

"That would seem to make sense, but that's not my job; it's the detectives' job."

That didn't add up. "But when you came over to Mugwort Manor this morning, you said that you were looking into it for yourself."

He smiled again. "I just made that up. I wanted to ask you to lunch, and I didn't know how to bring the subject up." He did his best impression of looking shy.

I forced a smile. "I've enjoyed having lunch with you, but I promised my aunts I wouldn't date for the first six months of my time here. I promised them I'd concentrate on the business. I'm already in trouble for agreeing to have lunch with you."

He looked disappointed, and I judged that as

genuine. But why? Was it simply disappointment that he couldn't question me at length? It seemed to me that the sergeant did have his own agenda for investigating this murder case.

We didn't speak after that, and a heavy, awkward silence fell over the table. Finally, I was saved when his phone vibrated. He said it was work and he had to leave at once, but for all I knew, it could've been his mother calling. I wasn't complaining—at least I had time to myself to drink my coffee in peace.

This certainly was a strange town, if you counted my aunts, the sergeant, and Lucas O'Callaghan. And then there were the guests, Paul and Linda Williams, who looked like vampires from an old black-and-white movie, and Marius Jones with his anger management issues.

I had left my car on the other side of town, because I had mistaken this restaurant for another. When I realised my mistake, I had decided to leave the car there and walk. I was used to walking long distances in Sydney, and didn't want to get out of the habit, and besides, I didn't know if I'd find parking easily outside this restaurant. On my walk back to my car, I saw Paul and Linda Williams in the butcher's.

I had to smile. *I bet they're ordering a cup of blood each*, I thought unkindly.

I walked along the street, looking in each window with interest. This was a tourist town, and since it was the beginning of summer, the place was bursting with tourists. There were plenty of cafés, and several interesting little gift shops. I saw to my delight there was a store with crystals and what looked like witchy supplies. I would have to return later and have a good look through it. I wanted to get back to the car in a hurry because a thunderstorm was imminent. The sky had been bright when I was heading to the restaurant, but now was black and threatening. I didn't want to get caught in a thunderstorm and get drenched.

I walked a little further, and was surprised to see Marius patting a large hairy dog. It looked like an Irish Wolfhound, but I couldn't be sure given that I had never seen one in the flesh. I stopped to say hello. "That's a beautiful dog," I said to the owner.

Marius agreed. "I pat him daily. I go for a walk this time every day. I miss my dog—he's with my wife at the moment. My ex-wife," he added pointedly. "That…" He uttered a string of nouns and adjectives that made me blush.

I smiled tightly and walked on, but one thing

was on my mind. Marius's shirt had dog hair all over it. The dog hair was flying off him so easily that I even thought I might sneeze. If Marius patted that dog every day, then he could well be the murderer.

CHAPTER 11

The lunch had been brief, and my aunts weren't expecting me back for an hour or so. Thunderstorm or not, I decided to drive to the lighthouse after which the town was named. I didn't intend to stay there long, but I wanted to see something of the town before I went back to the house and tackled the website.

As a child, I had been fascinated by the lighthouse, with its whale-watching area and the plaques telling of the shipwrecks on the rocks below.

I drove on for several minutes before I realised I had missed the turnoff to the lighthouse. I turned the car around. That was easier said than done. This was Aunt Dorothy's car, an old FJ Holden. It had probably been quite something in its day, but that was some years ago. It didn't have power steering and it was like driving a truck. My three-point turn descended into something like a fifteen-point turn on the narrow road, but finally I had the car pointed in the right direction.

I hadn't gone but a short distance when I heard a strange sound and felt a vibration. "Flat tyre!" I said to nobody in particular. I pulled the car off the road, and got out. Sure enough, one of the back tyres was as flat as a pancake, so flat it was sitting on the rim. I went to the back of the car and looked through the boot for a spare tyre, but then the rain began in earnest. Tiny little pieces of hail stung me, beating viciously against my face. The weather had suddenly turned icy cold, quite a contrast from the earlier pleasant warm morning. I moved things around, trying to reach for the spare. It didn't want to come, so I pulled it as hard as I could with both hands. Suddenly, it came away and I fell backwards into a puddle, the tyre on top of me.

From my position on the ground, I heard a car coming up behind me, and thought that I should've turned on my car's hazard lights. It was a pale coloured car and the rain would camouflage it to some degree. Luckily, the car behind me pulled over. I was surprised to see Lucas get out of it.

I struggled to my feet, letting the tyre fall onto the wet road. Lucas hurried over to me. "Flat tyre?"

I nodded, my teeth chattering. "Go and sit in the car, and I'll change it for you."

"Oh, um, you don't have to do that," I stuttered. He waved my concerns away, and then ripped off his leather jacket. "You're cold. Get in the car and I'll change the tyre." He threw his jacket over my shoulders.

I thanked him and hurried to the car. I sat there, in my passenger seat, huddling into the warmth of his leather jacket. It smelt like him, like rosemary and open log fires—and danger. My right eye twitched.

He tapped on the window and I jumped. I opened the door a little, mortified to see that he was completely drenched. "The spare tyre is flat, too," he said.

"Flat?" I echoed.

He nodded. "Yes, just as flat as the other tyre. Come on, I'll give you a lift back to Mugwort Manor."

I jumped out of my car and followed him to his hire car, the silver Porsche. "I'm sorry to drip water all over your car," I said. "Thanks so much for stopping to help me. I hope it's not out of your way to take me back home."

He started the engine and then shot a sideward glance at me. "That's where I'm headed, anyway. The Ambrosia Winery is back down that road. This is the road I take to travel between Mugwort Manor and the winery."

"Oh." I had a horrible thought. What if he thought I had deliberately punctured both tyres just to get a lift home with him? I was mortified.

I moved away from him, against the door, and didn't say another word until he pulled up on the road next to the flagstone pathway to the manor. I handed back his jacket and thanked him once more. "I'm so sorry you got wet. Thanks again," I said, and without waiting for him to say anything, I hurried up the flagstone path.

I rang the doorbell, and stood there shivering when I sensed movement behind me. I spun around to see Lucas. I hadn't even heard him approach. He handed my handbag to me. "You forgot this."

I was worried that he thought I did it deliberately, to cause more contact between us. "Thanks."

Just then, Aunt Dorothy opened the door.

"What happened? You two are drenched. Come in."

I hadn't expected Lucas to go inside, but he did.

"We have the fire going in the kitchen, because it's so cold all of a sudden," Dorothy said. "Come and warm yourself, Mr O'Callaghan."

I was surprised that Lucas agreed. "Now don't slip," Aunt Agnes said. "A handyman came earlier and used an extension ladder to tie plastic over the stained glass skylight, but it still leaked a little in the storm. We had to put all those plastic buckets under it."

The two of us followed Aunt Dorothy to the kitchen and stood in front of the fire. Aunt Maude took one look at us, left the room, and returned with two huge fluffy white towels.

Aunt Agnes was sitting at the kitchen table, sipping from a teacup. "How did you two get so wet?"

"I wanted to drive to the lighthouse, but I missed the turn. When I realised I'd missed the turn, I turned around, but then I got a flat. I pulled over but I had trouble getting the other tyre out. Then Mr O'Callaghan came along and found the spare tyre was just as flat as the first tyre. He gave me a lift home."

"That's very kind of you," Aunt Agnes said to Lucas.

Aunt Dorothy had turned on the coffee pot, and now was pouring two cups of coffee. She pulled chairs over to the fire for us and then handed us each a cup of coffee. Aunt Maude took the towels and hurried off in the direction of the laundry.

"I thought you were having lunch with Sergeant Carteron?" Aunt Agnes asked me.

I don't know why I felt guilty, but I did. Lucas showed no reaction. And why would he? It wasn't as if we were dating. I just had a simple silly little crush on him, that was all, and it's a wonder that I did, given his previous rudeness to me. Still, today he had been nothing but gentlemanly.

"He left early, a work matter, and since our lunch was brief, I thought I'd just pop out and have a look at the lighthouse," I explained.

"Did you get any information out of him?" Aunt Maude asked me.

I was worried that she asked in front of Lucas, but Aunt Agnes didn't rebuke her, so I figured it was all right to answer. "No, not really. He just asked a lot of questions about the three of you."

"What did he ask?" Aunt Agnes was suddenly alert.

"Just whether you'd ever had any dogs as pets, and how long you'd been living here, that sort of thing. He also asked if the guests had any pet dogs."

Aunt Dorothy tapped her chin. "Just the same as the detectives asked us."

I nodded. "He said the reason he was here this morning asking questions was simply a ruse to ask me out for lunch, but I figure that, in turn, was simply another ruse."

Lucas spoke for the first time. "Why would you say that?"

"Well, he obviously only asked me to lunch to ask me a lot of questions," I said. "Clearly he had his own agenda."

Lucas smirked.

"What do you find so funny about that?" I said, somewhat snappily.

Lucas waved his hand, gesturing up and down me. "Look at you! A man asked you on a date, and you think he had an ulterior motive. I don't think so."

I shifted in my seat, and avoided looking at him. Was that a compliment? For once, I was struck speechless.

Silence descended over the room for a moment, broken when Aunt Maude offered everyone a piece of carrot cake. "Was that all he asked?" she said once everyone had a piece of cake, a silver cake fork, and a delicate bone china plate.

"Yes, just questions like that, about the case." My voice trailed away.

"Did he ask any other questions? Anything at all?" Aunt Agnes asked.

"No, not really." I tried to recall. "Oh yes, he did ask how I felt about vampires."

"How you felt about vampires?" Lucas said, raising his eyebrows.

"Oh yes, and werewolves."

"Why would he ask such a thing?" Aunt Maude asked, but I saw Agnes shoot her a look, and she stopped speaking.

I shrugged. "Because he said he'd just bought a funny movie about vampires and werewolves, and he wanted me to go to his house to watch it sometime."

"What did you say?" Aunt Agnes asked me.

"I declined. I said that I only liked romantic comedies."

"Quite so," Aunt Agnes said firmly. "I can't bear to watch *The Walking Dead.*"

"There are no vampires or werewolves in *The Walking Dead*," Maude said. "They're zombies."

"No, they're not," Dorothy said. "They're not called zombies."

"Doesn't matter what they're called," Maude snapped at her. "Call them what you will, they're still zombies."

Lucas leaned forward, and spoke in such a low tone that I had to edge closer to hear his words. "I don't want to scare you, but please don't take any risks. I just can't shake off the feeling that you're in danger."

I shivered. "Do you mean I'm in danger, or my aunts are?"

Lucas shot a look at my aunts, but I could still hear them bickering behind me. "Possibly all of you, but you especially."

"Why? Why me?"

Lucas shook his head. "Just make sure you keep all the doors and windows locked. And don't date that sergeant again."

"It's none of your business who I date or don't date," I said angrily, but he ignored me, stood up and thanked my aunts for their hospitality.

Aunt Agnes pushed her chair back and made to stand, but clutched her lower back. "Thank you for bringing Valkyrie home safely."

"My pleasure." He nodded to me and took his leave out the back door.

I stood up. "I'd better have a warm shower and get changed."

"Good idea," Aunt Agnes said, "and then meet us back here in the kitchen. We need to increase the protection around the house. Before you go, what did that man whisper to you when he thought we weren't listening?"

I smiled. Nothing got past my aunts. "He said he thought we were all in danger, me especially." I thought I had better not mention that he told me not to date the sergeant.

If my aunts were concerned, they did not let it show.

"Exactly what did the sergeant say about vampires and werewolves?" Agnes asked me.

"Nothing much," I said, wondering why they were interested. "Just what I told you before. He only mentioned them once, and said he'd bought a movie about them, a funny one, made in New Zealand."

"I know that movie, but I can't remember the name," Aunt Dorothy said. "It was made by the same man who made that other famous New Zealand film. You know the one?"

Agnes and Maude shook their heads.

"I think the sergeant seems a bit too strange," Aunt Agnes said. "You're a big girl, Valkyrie, but I wouldn't like it if you went on another date with him."

"You don't have to worry about that," I assured her. "I told him I wouldn't."

I didn't know if it was my imagination, but all three appeared immeasurably relieved.

The storm was loud now. As I walked up the stairs, I could hear the hail on the roof. I was looking forward to my nice hot shower. I went to the long corridor and made to turn left to go to my bedroom, but I had taken only one step in that direction when I heard a sound to my right. At first I thought it was thunder, but it came again just after a boom of thunder. Surely two thunderclaps wouldn't come so close together.

I looked back down the stairs, but there was no sign of my aunts. I turned to the right in the direction of the forbidden room for the second time since I had to come to Lighthouse Bay.

My mouth was dry and my palms sweaty. I crept along, although the sound of the hail more than covered any noise I might make.

As soon as I turned the corner, again I saw that

red pulsating light. My heart nearly leapt out of my chest as I covered the last few yards at a sprint.

I put my ear to the door.

The noise was loud and clear. It was the sound of growling.

CHAPTER 12

I turned and ran. When I reached my bedroom, I locked the door behind me, my hand trembling on the door knob.

I stood there, shaking. Why were my aunts keeping a dog locked in a room? And more to the point, why was it such a secret? And why was there a red glow under the door? I supposed they might have a red light in there for some medical reason, but that was the least of my concerns.

Were my aunts somehow involved in the murder? They were certainly acting suspiciously.

I walked over to my bed and sat on it, and then realised I was wringing my hands. The police had found dog hair on the roof and in the tree. Could the murderer have somehow come into contact with the dog?

I crossed to the window and looked out. The landscape before me looked peaceful, pretty white cottages juxtaposed against freshly mown green lawns. From my elevated position, I could see the sea and the headland to the south. It was a pretty place, something one would find in ancient pastoral poetry, not the scene of a desperate murder. This was like something out of *The X-Files*.

I sighed and fetched my clothes for my shower. I debated asking my aunts about what was in that room, but I didn't quite have the courage, to be honest. If they were somehow involved in the man's murder, what would they do to me? I was sure they wouldn't harm me. Well, I wasn't one hundred percent sure, and so I decided I would keep what I knew to myself, and see how things unfolded.

I showered quickly, went back to my bedroom, and opened my little vial that contained a mixture of salt and agrimony, a strong protection. I put a few pinches of the mixture in my jeans pocket, and then I placed a eucalyptus leaf in each shoe. That was another protective measure.

I had already put a mixture of eggshell and crushed red brick dust across the windowsills and across the doorway both of my bedroom and my bathroom, on the night I arrived.

I walked back down the stairs in the direction of the kitchen, trying to keep my expression neutral. The storm had stopped. The weather was already warming up, the moisture of the storm causing the humidity to rise. Despite being on the coast, Lighthouse Bay was generally devoid of humidity, but at times like this, after rain, the humidity rose sharply.

The aunts had obviously fetched their own potions. "This is what we normally do for a thorough spiritual cleansing," Aunt Agnes said. "First we wash all the floors both upstairs and downstairs, with Van Van Oil in hot water."

I nodded. I myself used Van Van Oil. "Van Van Oil is a mixture of five African grasses," Aunt Agnes said, obviously taking my nodding as agreement rather than as an indication that I knew what Van Van Oil was. "It's a combination of citronella, palmarosa, ginger grass, vetiver, and lemongrass."

"And we sprinkle witches' salt all over the carpets," Aunt Maude added, "and then we vacuum it. Do you know what witches' salt is, Valkyrie?"

"It's salt mixed with ash, such as ash from the fire," I said.

All three aunts nodded. "We'll start with the floor wash and the vacuuming," Aunt Agnes said. "That will take us quite some time, but it will be easier with four of us to do the work. Then we'll take some white sage and walk through the house smudging it. We can also use eucalyptus oil. After we smudge the entire house, we'll go around and spray this Protection Oil." She indicated some plastic spray bottles on the kitchen table. "It's made from agrimony, rue, Black Snake Root, and sandalwood. After we do that, we'll go through the house with a singing bowl. We have several singing bowls. Have you used one before, Valkyrie?"

I had to admit that I hadn't.

Aunt Agnes tut-tutted. "A singing bowl raises the level of the vibrations and removes all the negative energy. Now with all these methods, Valkyrie, you probably already know to pay particular attention to the corners. Normally, we would need to leave the doors and windows open so the negativity could escape, but given what's happened, we'll have to be more cautious. We can open the windows upstairs, but we'll have to leave the front door locked. However, while you were having a shower, we opened the top of all the sash windows downstairs."

I nodded. They must have moved like lightning to open every sash window downstairs. After all, I hadn't taken long in the shower. They must have been fitter than they looked, which couldn't be hard, considering their fitness level looked to be zero on a scale of one to ten. Aunt Agnes was still talking. "Valkyrie, you start with your bedroom and your bathroom, but we'll do your corridor. After you do those two rooms, you start downstairs. Maude and Dorothy and I will do upstairs and when we're finished, we'll come downstairs and help you finish up there. How does that sound?"

It sounded like a lot of work, but I merely said, "Good. I suppose we start with the floor wash?"

"The vacuuming, actually." Aunt Agnes handed me a large glass bottle of witches' salt. "After you sprinkle that around, use that vacuum there." She pointed to a modern vacuum cleaner, quite an upmarket one. "When you finish that, then simply pour Van Van Oil into a bucket here and fill it with very hot water. There's a mop over there." She nodded to the bucket and mop nearby. "It's a microfibre mop, have you heard of those?"

"Yes," I said. "The fabric does the cleaning—you don't need any chemicals."

"Quite right." With that, the aunts and I headed for the stairs. I made my way through my bedroom and bathroom, and then through the rooms downstairs, throwing witches' salt all over the place. As I approached the place where the victim had landed on the parquetry floor, I dumped the remainder of the witches' salt on that very area.

By the time I had vacuumed the two rooms upstairs and every room downstairs, I was feeling a little tired. It didn't help that there was so much furniture around, so I had to keep plugging and unplugging the vacuum cleaner every few moments. I had to manoeuvre delicately around many pieces of furniture which were topped by what looked like valuable glassware.

When I had finished that, I gathered the buckets that were put under the hole in the roof, and took them to the laundry. I was surprised that the storm hadn't swept away the plastic cover over the skylight.

I tipped out the water, and then returned to the kitchen to fetch the Van Van Oil. I'd only had time to pour the hot water in the bucket, and then put in a measure of Van Van Oil, when the front doorbell rang.

I walked to the front door, wondering if the aunts would answer, but they were only halfway down the stairs. "You open it," Aunt Agnes called out.

I opened the front door to see a pizza delivery man standing there. "Mugwort Manor?" he said.

"I don't think we ordered pizza," I said. I looked behind me at my aunts. "Did we?"

"No, we didn't. Perhaps one of the guests did." Aunt Agnes addressed the man. "Do you have the name?"

He consulted his notes. "Marius Jones?"

"He's in cottage seven," Aunt Agnes said. "Just go around the back and you'll see a big brass seven hanging on the wall. That's him."

The pizza boy apologised and turned away, but Agnes called after him. "Those pizzas smell good. What sort are they?"

"Steak," he said.

He made to turn away again, but she asked another question. "Are those five pizzas all for him?"

The pizza boy nodded. Agnes shut the door.

The aunts exchanged glances. I suspected there

was a problem, but I had no idea what it was. "He must be having a party," I said.

"Maude, go out the back and see if there are any cars outside cottage number seven," Agnes ordered. Aunt Maude hurried off to do her bidding. "So, Valkyrie, how are you going down here?"

"Pretty good," I said. "I finished all the vacuuming, and now I'm about to wash the floors."

"I'm quite disturbed about this," Aunt Dorothy said.

"About what?" I asked her.

"The pizza man interrupting us while we were doing the house cleansing," Agnes said. "Some people read tarot cards, others do scrying, but the type of divination we do is one that takes signs from things around us. For example, if I'm always able to find a parking spot easily, I know that everything is open to me in my life at that time. However, if I have trouble and have to drive around for a while until I find one, I know there are blockages and obstacles in my life. That's probably not a very good example, but our family takes signs from everyday life. That's how we do our divinations."

"Yes, that was quite a common method of divination in the ancient world," I said, "such as observing the patterns or cries of birds flying. It was called *Augury*, but they also paid attention to what they called *Portents*, such as someone sneezing or tripping, or an everyday sort of thing. But what does that have to do with the pizza delivery?"

"It means that we were interrupted while doing a protective spell, and that's never a good thing."

"I thought we were just cleaning," I said, puzzled.

Aunt Agnes shook her head. At that moment, she looked powerful, younger, taller, somehow. I rubbed my eyes, thinking I must be overtired. "There is no such thing as *just cleaning* to a witch. Cleaning is a spiritual matter," she said in a high, clear voice. "In fact, most people know that clutter attracts negative energy. One should never have negative energy in one's own home. When you clean, work your intent into your cleaning. Today, we're working protection into our cleaning. Cleaning is a mundane work, but it's also a spiritual one. It has great spiritual importance. That's why we never use cleaners, not for the house at any rate. We use a local lady from town for the cottages."

I nodded. My aunts were certainly wise, and I could learn a lot from them. Now if only I could find out what was going on in that mysterious room.

Aunt Maude returned, breathless. "There are

no cars outside cottage seven," she said. "I stole a look through his window, and he was tucking into those pizzas. It looks as though he's going to eat them all himself."

The aunts looked at each other, something I was beginning to become accustomed to them doing. They were clearly keeping something from me, but what?

"Look, there's something I wanted to..."

The doorbell rang again. "Surely not the pizza boy?" I said.

Aunt Agnes marched past me and opened the door. "Hello?"

I peeped around her and saw a tall man.

"I'm James McPherson from The Sunbeam Insurance Company," he said, handing Agnes a card.

She pocketed the card, and said, "But you're a few hours early."

"I apologise. I did try to call, and I also emailed. I can come back later if that's more convenient. It's just that my earlier appointment finished faster than I anticipated, so I came straight over."

"No that's fine." Agnes motioned him inside.

"Is it all right if I give the boys the go ahead to go up on the roof?"

"Sure, send them right up."

He looked up at the skylight and whistled. "That's impressive. Did you get any further damage from that storm today?"

"No." Agnes shook her head. "Our handyman went up on the roof and fastened sheets of plastic as best he could. It did leak, but hopefully there's no damage. So what happens now? We're not used to insurance claims, so I don't really know the correct procedure."

"It's all quite straightforward," the man said. "It's a homicide case, and the police are involved. That will make your claim go through that much more smoothly. Do you have any photographs or any documents pertaining to the original stained glass?"

"Yes, we do. I have them out ready in the office. Dorothy, go and get them for the gentleman."

Dorothy hurried away. The man pointed to the floor. "Was this where the victim landed?"

Agnes assured him that it was.

"I'll organise some temporary glass as soon as possible just to make it all watertight, and then we'll look into replacing the actual stained glass itself."

"How long before you think you can insert the temporary glass?" Agnes said.

He shrugged. "It will be within five business days." He looked through the folder Dorothy had just handed him. "Excellent. This will do for now, but I'll be in touch. I'll just go and speak to my men. Good day, ladies."

Aunt Agnes locked the door behind him. "Do you see, Valkyrie? Two interruptions while we're doing a protection spell. That does not bode well. Anyway, what were you going to ask me?"

I had lost my courage. "I, um, nothing, nothing really."

She crossed her arms. "Now then, Valkyrie, I know that's not true. You had something to say to me. What is it?"

I took a deep gulp. "What's going on in the forbidden room?"

I heard Dorothy gasp behind me. "Why, that's just our private altar room, Valkyrie," Aunt Maude said.

Agnes shook her head. "Sisters, we knew we would have to tell Valkyrie."

Maude gasped. "But I thought we agreed we'd let her settle in first."

"She's obviously been snooping, so we need to tell her now. Valkyrie, this will come as quite a shock to you. You'll have trouble believing what we tell you, but I ask you to reserve judgement until we show you the contents of the room itself."

That did not sound good. What could possibly be in that room?

Aunt Agnes continued. "Valkyrie, I want you to promise me that you will not run away or run to your bedroom, but will right now accompany us to the room and see it for yourself, no matter how much you disbelieve us."

"Sure." I was intrigued, and a little scared. "What's in the room?"

"A werewolf."

CHAPTER 13

I wasn't sure I had heard correctly. "I'm sorry, I didn't quite hear what you said."

"A werewolf."

"What?"

"A werewolf. A Shifter. The human that becomes the wolf."

"It's not actually a werewolf," Aunt Maude said.

"One thing at a time," Agnes said. "I don't want to confuse her."

"You'll confuse her if you say it's a werewolf," Maude countered.

I clutched my throat. "A werewolf?"

All three aunts nodded. "Sort of," Aunt Maude muttered.

"But there's no such thing as werewolves."

"Tell that to the werewolf in the room." Aunt Agnes's voice was matter-of-fact. "Now, Valkyrie, you promised you would come with us to see the creature for yourself."

I tried to speak, but no words would come out. I stood frozen to the spot. What on earth were the aunts talking about? I figured they had found a large stray dog and thought it was a werewolf, but this meant they were all a little unhinged. I had given up my life in the city to come and work for my aunts, and now this? I always knew they were eccentric, but this was going too far.

"Follow us." Aunt Agnes walked up the stairs, followed by Maude and Dorothy. I brought up the rear.

"Don't be afraid. He's behind bars, and our magic contains him."

I was really concerned. Who could I call to get help for them? First I had to sort out the large stray dog.

Part of me was terribly excited that I would finally get to see inside the forbidden room, a room which had held such mystery for me as a child. As we approached the corridor, I could see the red light pulsating under the door. "Why is there a red glow under the door?" I asked Aunt Agnes.

"It's infrared light," she said. "It keeps him more docile."

I nodded. They really were buying into this werewolf thing, the poor old dears.

"Now before we show you, Valkyrie, I should say that you need to keep this a secret. I'm sure you won't go blabbing it all over town, of course, but I'm sure you can understand the need for secrecy."

"Yes," I said. "Your secret's safe with me." I wondered how I would be able to convince them that some hapless stray dog was in fact just that, and not a werewolf.

Aunt Agnes unlocked the door and flung it open. The aunts walked inside. One of them switched on the light. I gasped and clutched my throat. There, in front of me, was a man about my age, and he was naked.

"Let me out of here, you old hags," he said, and then let out a string of profanities that made me blush.

"You said it was a dog, but he's a man!" I said in horror. "You've kidnapped a man! You could go to jail for years and years for doing that!" I was absolutely horror stricken.

"We didn't say there was a dog here," Aunt Dorothy explained patiently. "We said it was a werewolf. This is a werewolf."

"Sort of," Aunt Maude muttered again.

"He's just a man," I said, aghast. "You have to let him go. He's not a wolf. Can't you see he's a man?" I found myself growing increasingly agitated. Why wouldn't they listen to me? I would have to go straight to the police.

"I know it's hard for you, Valkyrie," Aunt Agnes said in a kindly tone, "but surely you know that werewolves look like humans most of the time? Don't you know what a werewolf is, dear?"

"But, but…" I sputtered.

"She needs him to change," Maude said.

I agreed with that, at least. "Yes, he could do with some clothes."

The aunts shook their heads sadly. "Valkyrie, you have so much to learn. When we say change, we don't mean change clothes." The aunts chuckled as if I had made a huge joke.

"He'll change into a werewolf," Aunt Agnes said, throwing some red powder at the poor man.

"What did you do that for?" I said.

"Prepare yourself to meet the werewolf," Aunt Agnes said dramatically.

I turned away to look at Agnes, and when I turned back, there was a giant creature in the cage. I was in disbelief. "How did you do that?" It didn't seem real—it couldn't be real. There was at once a chemical smell in the room, but I didn't have time to consider that, as the creature flung itself at the bars and barred its teeth at me. I jumped backwards. For a moment, I stared at the long hair covering the creature, his broad and protruding eyebrow ridges, the receding forehead.

"Now do you believe us?" Aunt Agnes said.

That was the last thing I remembered.

I woke up on the hard floor with a pillow under my head. "I had a bad dream," I said, looking up at the aunts who hovered over me, one patting my cheek, and the other two patting my hands. "We didn't think you'd take it this badly," Aunt Dorothy said. "You fainted."

"I had a bad dream," I said again, pleased to hear my voice was a little stronger.

"It wasn't a dream, Valkyrie," Aunt Agnes said. She stepped aside, and I saw the giant hairy creature growling, and pacing up and down.

I did the breathing technique a therapist had taught me when I had suffered anxiety back in my university days. I took a long, slow breath through my nose and counted to three before exhaling through my mouth until my lungs were empty. It was a simple technique, but it had worked for me previously.

This time, it didn't seem to help. "Werewolves are real?" I said. I couldn't bring myself to believe it, even though I could see the evidence before me with my very own eyes.

"Agnes, throw some of the powder on him to make him turn back into a human," Aunt Dorothy said.

"Now Dorothy, it's not a party trick," Agnes said in a scolding tone.

"I feel sick," I said as a wave of nausea hit me.

"Here, open your mouth."

I did as Agnes bid, and she dropped some liquid into my mouth. It did seem to work; I felt well enough to prop myself onto my elbow. The shock was so great, it had given me an instant stress headache.

"Now we need to talk about why we have this creature in our room," Agnes said, "but please stay here until you're absolutely convinced that this creature is a Shifter."

"I'm convinced," I said weakly.

The aunts helped me to my feet, and guided me

outside the room. Aunt Agnes locked the door. "It can't get out of there, can it?" I asked, worried. "Was that what killed that man?" The realisation hit me like a block of concrete. It suddenly all made sense. The animal hairs the police collected and the fact that someone—something—had the strength to carry the body of a heavy man up a tree and onto the high roof.

"We'll explain it all in the kitchen," Agnes said.

I don't know how I made it to the kitchen. My legs were like jelly. I wondered how the aunts had such presence of mind not to freak out at the sight of a werewolf. "I can't believe werewolves exist," I said over and over again like a mantra.

I was sitting at the kitchen table, and Aunt Maude was busy making me a hot chocolate. "I'm going to put in several spoons of sugar, for the shock," she said.

She had it in front of me in no time at all. I thanked her, and sipped it. The sugary goodness ran through my veins, reviving me somewhat.

"It's not like women of our bloodline to be shocked at the sight of such things," Aunt Agnes said. "Maude, pour Valkyrie a glass of that wine, the special wine."

Maude produced a glass of red wine, and again,

I didn't even know how she had time to prepare it. Everything seemed to happen in a lightning fast manner.

"Why do you have that werewolf captive?" I asked them.

Maude sighed dramatically. "It's not a werewolf."

"I should've thought it was obvious why we have it captive," Agnes said. "Aunt Maude, she can call it werewolf if she wants. It makes it simpler."

I was too stressed to care about the technicalities of the thing's name. I drank some more of the hot chocolate and then took a sip of wine. The combined taste in my mouth was pleasant. It reminded me of a brand of red wine I used to buy that had heavy chocolate notes. I rubbed my forehead, trying to focus on the situation at hand. "I'm still in shock," I said. "A werewolf! I've actually seen a live werewolf." I felt hysteria rising in me, so I poured another glass of wine. That seemed to help, so I drank half a glass in one go.

"To answer your question," Aunt Agnes said, "and remember, Valkyrie, anything we have kept from you was to spare you the shock of finding out. We didn't want to scare you, dear."

Before I could respond, she pressed on. "This Shifter took part in killing that poor man, but he has an accomplice, and we're holding him in that cage until he tells us the name of his accomplice."

"You mean there are two of them?" I said, terrified. "Two werewolves?"

"Exactly," Dorothy said. "Two Shifters, and this one's not talking."

"Yes, of course, you can't turn him over to the police." It was as if I heard someone else talking. I was surprised I had the presence of mind even to think of such a thing, given the shock flooding over me.

And then something occurred to me. "Was it trying to kill one of you?"

"Oh no, dear," Agnes said. "I think it's all to do with the winery, like you said. But still, we can't have an angry Shifter running around Mugwort Manor, now can we?"

"No, I suppose not. You'll have to bear with me, Aunts. I've always believed in fairies, but I've never thought werewolves were real."

"There are a lot more real things than you imagined," Agnes said. "You're taking it well now, dear."

"The wine helps." I drank the rest of my glass, and instantly refilled it. "I don't know if I should be drinking so much wine when I've had such a terrible shock."

"It's very low alcohol," Agnes said. "It's special wine."

"Special? How?" The wine certainly tasted different, and nice too. Somehow it made me feel good inside.

Aunt Agnes smiled. "Now that's a conversation for another day. Suffice to say, we have a murderous Shifter trapped in the cage, and he has not as yet told us who his accomplice is."

"Are Shifters vicious?" I asked her. "Are they like the werewolves on TV, that can't control themselves and run around ripping out everyone's throats? They have to be locked up every full moon or they're very dangerous."

"You'll find that allegedly mythical creatures have been quite wrongfully depicted by Hollywood," Aunt Agnes said with disgust. "No, of course they can control themselves."

"So have you known for a long time that werewolves exist?" I asked her.

She nodded. "We'll talk about this in more

depth at some other time. I have to make one thing clear. We have to be quite alert. The Shifter's accomplice doesn't know he's here—they don't have an overly developed sense of smell, or anything like that. So we're safe in that regard. But meanwhile, Valkyrie, be alert and keep your eyes open. Someone you've met since you came to town is a Shifter and a murderer."

The nausea came back, and I leaned forward. Mercifully, it passed after a few moments.

"Are we going to tell her he's not exactly a werewolf?" Maude asked.

It was all going downhill. "What is it then?" I asked.

"I didn't want to confuse you, dear. Think of it as a werewolf if it helps," Aunt Agnes said kindly, while glowering at Maude. "It's a Shifter all right, but it's a Yowie."

"A Yowie?" I squealed. "As in Indigenous Australian legend? I thought they were mythical creatures, but not Shifters."

"There are many Shifters in Indigenous Australian legends," Agnes said. "Most Aussies think of the Yowie as a humanoid creature that walks upright, and looks something like a tall and very shaggy man, like the Australian version of the Sasquatch. And a Yowie itself isn't a Shifter, any more than a wolf itself is a Shifter. Most Yowies are gentle and shy, but the Shifter Yowies can have dreadful temperaments, just like werewolves."

I tried hard to process the information. "I've heard stories that truck drivers on the mountain road from Colo to Bulga pulled over to catch some sleep, and woke up to find a Yowie jumping up and down in front of the truck," I said, "and I've heard stories that there are Yowies out near Mudgee, but I thought perhaps the people who reported them were drunk, or some such thing."

"No one thinks Yowies are real, of course, dear," Dorothy said, "not until they meet one."

Agnes shook her finger at her. "In 1977, Sydney University sent a team to the hills behind the Warkworth Mine in the Hunter Valley to investigate Yowies. And many people have seen them."

"The noise it made, that screeching sound— why can't we hear it out here?"

"The room is soundproofed, to a degree," Agnes said. "You'd need to put your ear to the door to hear anything."

I didn't like to admit that I had done just that.

Then something occurred to me. "How did you manage to catch it?"

"We're powerful witches," Dorothy said, narrowing her eyes.

I thought there was more to it, but I'd had enough of a shock for one day—for one lifetime.

CHAPTER 14

*T*hadn't been productive for the rest of the day. I was still coming to terms with the fact that there was such a thing as a werewolf, or a Yowie Shifter, to be precise. It was beyond belief, but I had seen the creature with my very own eyes. I had always believed in the supernatural—after all, I practised witchcraft, but I had always imagined that my spells were simply the result of focus, of something akin to positive thinking. Many people believed in the Law of Attraction, and I had always thought my witchcraft was the result of that. Shifters were one step beyond that. Did this mean that monsters did exist, after all?

My aunts had assured me that there was absolutely no way that the Shifter could escape from the room, but it made my flesh crawl to think that a murdering Shifter was under the same roof. Not surprisingly, I was unable to sleep. I had finally drifted off to sleep, and then had awoken just after midnight. Any further attempts to sleep had proven completely futile. I tried to read a book on my iPad, but I jumped at every little sound. There was an owl hooting outside my window, but my imagination had me thinking it was a werewolf.

I needed to go to the bathroom, and that meant I had to leave the safety of my bedroom. I spent about fifteen minutes debating what to do, but I had no choice—I simply had to use the bathroom.

I plucked up my courage and pushed the dresser away from the front of the door. I carefully opened the door, jumped into the corridor, locked the door behind me, and then made a mad dash across the corridor to the bathroom. I flicked on the light, shut the door behind me, and locked it.

Moments later, I washed my hands and looked at myself in the mirror. "What am I going to do now?" I asked myself aloud. The thought occurred to me that as my aunts were powerful enough witches to catch a werewolf, then they were powerful enough to contain it as long as they wanted. That was an encouraging thought.

With that in mind, I now felt brave enough to go down to the kitchen and make some hot chocolate. That would help me sleep, and my stomach was rumbling. I had been so upset to find that werewolves existed that I hadn't been able to eat much dinner at all.

I tiptoed down the stairs, careful not to wake my aunts, and then walked into the kitchen. I turned on the light. It's amazing how light dispels fears so readily. Whatever was lurking in the dark would still be there, but the light was somehow comforting and encouraging.

I turned on the electric kettle, and then fetched the hot chocolate powder and the sugar from the pantry. I found the biggest coffee mug I could, and spooned both in. I would have liked to sit in the kitchen and sip the hot chocolate, but I decided that I would prefer to be in my locked bedroom.

I poured the hot water and the almond milk onto the hot chocolate powder, and stirred it well. Large mug in hand, I intended to head back to my bedroom, and that's when I saw it.

I screamed and dropped my mug on the floor.

It seemed to happen in slow motion, the face fading from the window, the shards of ceramic splintering and spreading all over the floor.

Within seconds, my aunts arrived. It must have been the shock that made me think no time had passed. There simply hadn't been enough time for them to get there so quickly.

"What happened?" Aunt Agnes said.

"Is that werewolf, um, Yowie still locked in the room?" I asked her.

"I'm sure he is," she said, "but Maude's checking on him now."

Aunt Maude appeared seconds later and gave the thumbs up.

"What did you see?" Agnes asked me.

Before I could answer, there was a loud knock on the back door. "It's Lucas O'Callaghan. Is everyone all right? I heard a scream."

"He couldn't have heard me from his cottage," I said. "Is he a Shifter, too? Do they have special hearing?"

Agnes shook her head. "No."

"No, he's not a Shifter, or no, they don't have special hearing?"

"No to both," she said firmly.

I wanted to ask how she knew, but he knocked on the door again and called out.

To my horror, Aunt Agnes opened the door. For

all I knew, he could be the murderer. My aunts had to be more careful.

Lucas walked into the room, looking calm and collected, in stark contrast to the urgency I'd heard in his voice only moments earlier. "What happened?" he asked in a composed but commanding tone.

"I saw something at the window," I said, pulling my thin bathrobe around me.

He stepped towards me and I involuntarily took a step backward. "What was it?" he asked.

I thought it strange that he said, 'What was it?' rather than, 'Who was it?' Surely the implication would be that I saw a person at the window. At any rate, I had seen what looked like the Yowie Shifter, but I could hardly tell him that.

"I think it was a man," I said, "a tall man. I saw the expression on his face and his eyes looking at me, and he had a lot of hair." I gave Aunt Agnes a look as I said it and wiggled my eyebrows at her, trying to give her the hint.

She kept her expression neutral, and asked, "Did you recognise him?"

I shook my head. "It happened so fast. He vanished in an instant."

"Could it have been Paul Williams?" Lucas asked me. "He has a lot of hair."

"No, this man seemed to have facial hair, although I can't be sure," I said, giving Aunt Agnes another significant look.

Agnes turned to Lucas. "Did you see anyone out there?"

"No I didn't, but I was in a hurry to get here when I heard Pepper scream. Perhaps I should go outside now and have a scout around."

"I'd rather you didn't," she said. "There could be more than one of them."

Lucas appeared to be thinking that over, but he finally agreed. "We need to call the police."

At first, Aunt Agnes did not appear keen to alert the police, and I figured that was because she had a Shifter in a cage in an upstairs room. However, she agreed readily enough. I made myself busy cleaning up the mess on the floor while Aunt Dorothy called the police, and Aunt Maude declared she would make everyone some hot chocolate.

The five of us sat around the table in uncomfortable silence, waiting for the detectives. They arrived five or so minutes later, but it seemed like an age.

Aunt Agnes showed them straight into the kitchen.

"Did you recognise the person?" Detective Anderson said, scribbling in his notepad. "Age? Gender? Height? Anything you can tell me."

I held up my hand. "He was about so high, and he had a lot of hair."

"So definitely a man?"

I nodded. "Yes, a man, but the fact that he had a lot of hair and was very tall is all I really know, because I only saw him for a split second staring through the window at me."

"Are you definitely sure you saw someone and it wasn't just a trick of the light?" Detective Banks asked me.

I was a little annoyed. "I am one hundred percent sure I saw a man at that window, Detective," I said, unable to keep the irritation out of my voice. "I looked straight into his eyes."

"Sure, we just have to ask," he said. "Anything else at all?"

"No, nothing. It was all over quite quickly."

"We'll have the police vehicle make more frequent patrols from now on," Anderson said.

"Could it have been an attempted burglary?" Lucas asked them. Without waiting for an answer, he turned to me. "There was an attempted burglary at the winery today, in broad daylight."

"Did they get anything?" Aunt Agnes asked him.

"Not as far as I know. The managers were home when it happened and they didn't see or hear anything, but considerable damage was done to some of the equipment."

All the aunts gasped, and their hands flew to their throats.

"Don't worry, ladies," Detective Anderson said. "Like I said, we'll increase the patrols past your house. It was likely vandalism, not an attempted burglary, at the winery."

"Will you still be able to produce your wine?" Aunt Agnes asked Lucas. Before he could answer, she continued. "First your wine scientist is murdered, and now your equipment is smashed. And of course your uncle died. Could he have been murdered, too? Someone is going to great lengths to shut down your winery."

Detective Anderson held up his hands. "Now, Miss Jasper, let's not jump to any conclusions. There have been burglaries all over town in the last week, mostly jewellery, small stuff."

"But you just said it wasn't a burglary as such," I pointed out. "You said it was vandalism."

"Quite so, quite so, but Mr O'Callaghan's managers haven't had a chance to go through the inventory. As far as we know, nothing of any significance was stolen. Anyway, the uniformed officers are looking into that."

"But surely it's part of the homicide investigation?"

He did not appear annoyed by my question. "If it is, then the uniformed officers will pass the information along to us and we will duly investigate."

"Do you have any new information on Talos Sparkes's murder?" Lucas asked him.

"We've analysed the hair we found around the base of the tree," the detective said.

"That reminds me," I said after I sipped some hot chocolate, "I saw Marius Jones patting a large grey dog today. He mentioned he pats that dog every day on his daily walk. It was quite a hairy dog, and I noticed he had hair all over his clothes."

The detective did not appear interested, but nevertheless scribbled in his notepad. "Could you please describe the dog? What breed was it?"

"I think it was an Irish Wolfhound," I said. "I

can't be sure. It was very tall and shaggy and sort of had the body shape of a greyhound only much bigger and taller, with lots of hair."

"Thanks for that." The detective shut his notepad.

"Does that description match the dog hair found?"

The detective shook his head. "I'm afraid I can't divulge that information. I can, however, tell you that we checked all dogs in town and haven't found a match for this particular dog."

It was then the penny dropped, and I felt like an awful fool. Of course the hair was from the Yowie. How could I have forgotten that fact? Call it shock, I suppose, but really I should've put two and two together. They had found Yowie hair, of that I was fairly certain.

Detective Anderson spoke. "Detective Banks and I will have a look outside, so don't be disturbed if you see lights out there. We'll say our goodbyes now, but we'll have a look around outside before we go. So it was that window there?"

I had already told him that, but I nodded. "And what were you doing again when you noticed the man looking at you?"

"I was making hot chocolate," I said. "I couldn't

sleep, what with everything that's happened. I had a full cup of hot chocolate, and was going to my room when I saw him looking at me. I got such a shock, I dropped my cup." I'd already told him that, but I suppose detectives like to ask several times to cross check their information.

"What are you doing here, sir?" Detective Banks asked Lucas.

"I heard Miss Jasper scream," he said.

"None of the other guests heard her scream," Banks said evenly, "or if they did, they didn't respond." He fixed Lucas with a look that could only be interpreted as accusing. I wondered if he suspected Lucas was the one looking through the window.

The detective turned to me. "How long after you screamed did Mr O'Callaghan arrive?"

I shook my head. "I can't be sure, but my aunts got here first and then Mr O'Callaghan."

"I couldn't sleep either," Lucas said. "I had fallen asleep watching TV, and then woke up in my chair. I got up to turn off the TV and as I did, I heard Miss Jasper scream."

The detective nodded. He appeared to accept the story, but I for one didn't. There was an obvious hole in the story. First of all, he said that he couldn't sleep, but also he said he had fallen asleep watching TV. It was impossible to do both. Was I just being overly picky because I didn't like the man? Sure, I had a crush on him, but that didn't mean I liked him.

The detectives walked out the back door, followed by Lucas. I looked at Aunt Agnes, but she shook her head. She walked over to me and patted me on my shoulder, and said loudly, "You've had quite a few shocks since you arrived here, dear." She leaned closer and said in a hushed tone, "Don't say a word about what you saw until we know the detectives have gone."

I was on my second cup of hot chocolate before the lights from the detectives' torches stopped flashing around behind the house. Aunt Agnes went to the front window to make sure they had driven away.

"It's all clear now," she said upon her return. "Did you see a person or a Shifter, Valkyrie?"

"A Shifter for sure," I said. "There was no mistaking it. It was tall and hairy, and had the face of an animal and a face of a human at the same time."

The aunts exchanged glances. "Why wouldn't someone snoop around in human form?" I asked them. "I mean, Yowies can hardly be common, so you wouldn't think one would risk being seen, even if no one would believe the person who reported seeing it."

"I'm afraid that whoever it is knows we would recognise him in his human form," she said. "And it could well be a female. You can't tell the difference between a male and a female Shifter just by looking at their faces."

I was suddenly deathly afraid. "Do you think it knows you have its accomplice locked up in your house?" I asked her.

"No, definitely not," Aunt Agnes said, although I could sense uncertainty in her voice. "This all revolves around Lucas O'Callaghan."

"Sure," I said. "I figured that out for myself. It seems fairly likely now that Lucas's uncle was murdered, and the murderer threw the victim at his feet moments after he arrived in town, and now his wine making equipment is vandalised. That means that someone's trying to shut down his winery. At least, that's how it's beginning to look to me."

All the aunts nodded. "That's what we're thinking too," Aunt Dorothy said. "The werewolf is looking for his or her partner in crime, and looking all around here for any clues, but has no idea that the three of us were the ones who captured the Shifter. After all, they think we're just harmless old ladies."

I had always thought they were harmless old ladies, but now I wasn't so sure. The three of them sat there, clicking away with their knitting needles, reminding me of the three Fates of ancient Greece who spun, measured, and cut threads to determine the fortunes of humankind.

"Are you able to make the Shifter tell you who it is?" I asked the aunts.

"We've been trying," Aunt Agnes said with a sigh of exasperation, "but this one is quite resilient."

"What do you mean *this one?*" I asked her. "Have you had other Shifters locked up there before?"

Aunt Agnes's eyes flickered from side to side. "That's a conversation for another time, dear."

I rubbed my temples. She had said that to me more than once, and it was a little frustrating. It was like being told things would be explained to me when I grew older. I'd had enough of that as a child.

Something else occurred to me. "I don't think

Lucas O'Callaghan could have heard me scream from there. Do you think he's the Shifter?"

"Of course not. We've told you that before. O'Callaghan is not a Shifter," Aunt Agnes said firmly.

"But how can you be so sure?" I asked her. "If you have powers to detect Shifters, then surely you could find the partner of the one you have locked up."

All three shook their heads. "No, we don't have those powers," Aunt Dorothy said. "It would be good if we did."

"So how do you know Lucas isn't a Shifter?" I asked them.

"I told you, dear," Aunt Agnes said patiently, "that's a conversation for another time. Meanwhile, I'll ask you to take our word for it that Lucas O'Callaghan isn't a Shifter."

I held up my hands in surrender. "Okay then, you win—I will. But how do you explain that he heard me scream? That seems impossible."

"Sound carries strangely in this area," Aunt Agnes said. "He doesn't have special Shifter hearing, if that's what you're thinking. Plus, we've already told you that Shifters don't have special hearing."

"If you say so," I said. "I think I need some Advil."

"You don't need some Advil," Aunt Dorothy said over the top of her knitting. "You need some of the special wine from the Ambrosia Winery."

"I'm not used to drinking so much alcohol," I protested.

"Nonsense, my dear," Aunt Agnes said brusquely. "This family has a high tolerance for alcohol, and besides, as we've already told you, this wine is very low in alcohol. It is, however, very high in vitamins and minerals, and exceptionally high in iron. It's just what you need. And have you ever heard of people drinking stout for their health?"

"This isn't stout, is it, though?" I asked her. "I thought stout was some sort of beer."

"Yes, of course it is," Aunt Dorothy said. "That was just an example. This is special wine which is more like a vitamin and mineral supplement in liquid form." She poured me half a glass of wine and watched me while I drank it. "It's medicinal," she added.

I did drink it, but I wondered how I would get out of drinking so much alcohol in the future. My three aunts seemed to be heavy wine drinkers, and it couldn't be good for them. I certainly didn't want to head down that road. Nevertheless, I had to admit that I always felt immeasurably better after drinking the wine. Perhaps there was some truth to their words after all.

"Yes, this must be a horrible shock for you, Valkyrie. Now as to your earlier question, we're working on getting that Shifter to tell us where his accomplice is."

"Can't you use Compulsion Oil, Bend Over Oil, or something like that on him?" I asked them.

"Yes we've done all that, and Tell the Truth Oil, too," Aunt Agnes said. "We've gone through quite a lot of liquorice root and calamus root."

"We won't be safe until the other Shifter's caught, will we?" I asked them.

They did not respond, and that was an answer in itself.

CHAPTER 15

 was sitting at a local cafe. The aunts had shooed me out of the house, saying they thought I should get out and drink some coffee to wake me up, but I didn't trust them, not one bit. I knew they were up to something, but what?

And so I sat at the café, drinking a long black, trying to wake up after my lack of sleep the previous night, and wondering what my aunts were doing in my absence.

I started to feel a little human after my double shot long black, so I ordered a sandwich. I looked around the cafe. It was entirely decorated in pink. All the chairs were pink; the walls were pink, and the fake plastic flowers on every table were pink. Clearly, pink was someone's favourite colour. As I continued to look around the room, I caught the eye of Linda Williams. She shot me a smile and walked over.

"May I join you?" she asked me.

"Sure." I gestured to the chair opposite. She was still smiling; I didn't know why. She had certainly not been overly friendly to me previously.

"Paul said you saw an intruder last night," she said, wasting no time coming to the point.

"Yes, I did. How did he know?"

She shrugged, and looked unconcerned. "No idea, I didn't ask him. Did you see who it was?"

I shook my head. "I could tell it was a man, that's all. I only got a brief glimpse."

The waitress came over and deposited my sandwich in front of me. She shot Linda an enquiring look. "Have you moved to this table, Madam?"

"Yes," she said, not even looking at the waitress. I wondered why she was turning her charm on me. Clearly, she wanted something. I decided just to wait and play it by ear. Sooner or later, she would show her hand.

"So you said you moved to Lighthouse Bay to help your aunts in the business," she said, eyeing me speculatively.

"Yes."

She arched her eyebrows. "There wasn't anyone else they could ask? I mean, with your degree in, um, what was it in again? English literature? Journalism?"

"Classical Literature," I supplied.

She nodded. "Quite so. Wasn't there anyone else they could ask?"

I shook my head. "It's a family thing, I'm sure. They wanted me to move in with them, and I'm the only family they have. They're the only family I have."

She drummed her fingers on the table, a gesture of impatience, or so I thought. Her face was impossibly pale and she hadn't used blush. I wondered if she normally lived in a cold climate. "I hope you didn't have to leave a good job." She said it as a statement rather than a question.

I answered, anyway. "No, I didn't have a job at all," I said. "That's why I jumped at the chance to move here."

"And how awful for you witnessing a murder on your very first day."

"Well, I didn't actually *witness* it," I said, eyeing her warily. I didn't know where these questions were headed. Still, she seemed to relax and I wondered what I could possibly have said to put her mind at rest.

Her food arrived, a huge steak. She cut into it greedily, and I saw that it was rare. She must have noticed me looking, because she gave an apologetic laugh. "I'm afraid I have a ferocious appetite. My husband always lectures me about it. I can eat a large juicy steak faster than most men can."

I tried to laugh, but it came out more as a choking sound. Come to think of it, Marius Jones had eaten five steak topped pizzas all by himself. Was he a werewolf? Were they both werewolves?

I sat there watching her devour her steak, while I nibbled delicately at my cheese and lettuce sandwich.

The waitress returned to ask if we would like more drinks, and we both declined, but as she turned away, I saw her face freeze and then she broke out into a smile. I followed her gaze, and it alighted on none other than Lucas O'Callaghan.

She rushed over to him. The movement was enough to draw Linda's attention, and at once a scowl covered her face.

I watched as another waitress walked over to Lucas. They spoke for a moment and the two waitresses left. He walked over to our table. "Good morning, ladies."

We both nodded. "I hope you had no more trouble last night?" he asked me.

I shook my head, wondering if I had lettuce stuck to my teeth. "No, none," was all I said, covering my mouth with my hand in an attempt to look pensive rather than looking like I was hiding stray bits of lettuce.

"Mrs Williams, did you hear anything last night just after midnight?" he asked Linda.

She shook her head, and then sawed viciously at her steak. He smiled tightly and walked away. I watched him as he ordered at the register, and realised he was getting takeaway.

"I hope you don't think I'm prying," I said, not really caring whether or not she thought so, "but I've noticed that you don't seem too fond of Mr O'Callaghan."

Linda chewed her mouthful, her eyes darting around the room. She seemed to be deciding whether or not to tell me something. "Well, it's like this. I dated his uncle some years ago, and it didn't end well."

"Really? Do go on."

She hesitated, and again shot me that

speculative look. "I've been coming to Lighthouse Bay on vacation ever since I was a teenager. I used to come with my parents. I didn't stay at Mugwort Manor; I stayed at various places, all of which have now closed. Did you know I only met my husband five years ago?"

I shook my head. "No, I didn't know."

"I met Henry Ichor about fifteen years ago," she said. "I had a mad crush on him, all the girls in town did. He had some sort of animal magnetism. I could hardly take my eyes off him." She lowered her voice, and nodded in Lucas's direction. "He looks so much like him. He's very attractive, don't you think?"

"He's good looking, all right," I said, "but he seems awfully conceited and arrogant."

She nodded. "Henry was the same. He told me at the beginning, when we started dating, that it wasn't going to be serious, that he had no intention of marrying me. I should've listened to him, but I thought I would be the one to change him. He made it clear that he was not interested in settling down, but he was just so attractive." She stopped speaking and shook her head.

"So you broke up?" I prompted.

"Yes. I was furious. That man broke my heart.

And to add insult to injury, I knew he dabbled in the stock market, and I asked him for a tip. He told me he was currently investing in invisibility technology."

"Gosh!" I said, rather too loudly. It was all too much—first werewolves, and now invisibility? This was nuts.

Linda laughed. I noticed she had rather long, pointy teeth. "Nothing paranormal, I can assure you. It's all done with cameras, a series of cameras and monitors woven into a cloak. The cameras are shooting what's behind you, and that's displayed on monitors in the front of the cloak. It's not real invisibility, but it's enough to fool the naked eye."

"So, your shares became worthless?" I guessed.

She shook her head. "No, I sold them and now they're worth a small fortune."

I frowned. "If you don't mind me saying so, that doesn't make sense. You don't like Henry because he advised you to buy shares that are now worth a fortune?"

She waved her fork at me. "He didn't explain it to me, that was the problem. I asked him time and time again to explain it to me and he didn't, so I ended up thinking it was all a scam. I'm upset about that, but he did break my heart."

"But he told you he wasn't interested in a long-term relationship," I said.

She narrowed her eyes. "It's hard to explain to someone else. I guess you just had to be there. I always felt he led me on, but I just couldn't resist him. At any rate, it's a good thing he died overseas while I was in this country, otherwise I'm sure the police would think I had a hand in it."

"But he wasn't murdered, surely?" I said, surprised.

She stabbed another piece of steak, and lifted it halfway to her mouth. "He was a healthy man," she said. "If he wasn't murdered, then it was an accident, and if it was an accident, then it could have been a murderer trying to make it look like an accident."

I tried to follow her line of reasoning, and wondered whether it was idle speculation, or whether she actually knew something. I felt uneasy with the woman, and there was no mundane, practical reason as to why I felt that way.

I looked up to see someone handing Lucas a package of takeaway food, and a large polystyrene cup of coffee or some liquid. This time, he left the room without so much as acknowledging our presence.

Linda noticed him go. "I tell you, if I wasn't married, I'd be throwing myself at that hottie. There's just something about him. He takes after his uncle in that regard. Speaking of that, I'm going to pop out to the winery after lunch."

I muttered something, and watched Lucas walk along the street. I wondered if he was eating steak, too. My aunts were so sure he wasn't a werewolf, but they wouldn't tell me why. I had no doubt they possessed information that I was not party to. I knew they weren't sharing everything with me at this time. What did they know about Lucas O'Callaghan?

After lunch, I decided to walk through town and do some window shopping. I was already beginning to adjust to the quieter pace of life here. I had initially feared I would become bored, but given what had happened since I arrived, I doubted that would be possible.

I wanted to buy a little gift for my aunts. I hadn't bought one in Sydney because I had to cram all my possessions into my luggage for the plane. I didn't know what they liked, but as they were always knitting, I figured they would like some wool.

I walked along the street, looking for a wool shop or a craft shop. I found one readily enough.

The door was shut. It was also heavy, as I discovered when I tried to push it open. I was immediately hit in the face with a blast of icy air. It was such a contrast from the outside air that I shivered. The air was strong with the cloying scent of frangipani, jasmine, lavender, and a few other fragrances I couldn't quite identify.

"Can I help you?" a disembodied voice asked me.

"I'm looking for a gift for my aunts," I said, looking around and seeing the assistant. "They're all very keen knitters, so I thought I should buy them some nice wool. Do you have any unusual wool?"

"Are they working on any projects at the moment?" she asked me over the top of a magazine.

"I'm afraid I couldn't say," I said. "Quite sadly, I'm no good at knitting."

"Practice makes perfect," she said, setting down her magazine. "We do have this lovely Merino wool here."

I followed her to the side wall, where she picked up a skein of wool and handed it to me.

"Oh, it's so soft," I said, "and it's beautiful. It's sort of iridescent."

She nodded. "It *is* expensive, but you really can't go past superfine Merino wool as a gift to knitters. What colours do your aunts like?"

I bit my lip. "I'm not really sure. I've been away for years. I've just come back to live with my aunts."

"You're Valkyrie Jasper, aren't you?" she said with renewed interest.

"Yes," I said, not bothering to tell her my name was Pepper. I waited for her to say something else, but she did not. "Maybe I should buy some colourful wool?"

"I have some hand-dyed Merino wool," she said proudly. "It's hand dyed with vegetable dyes. Which one do you think your aunts would like?"

I eventually settled on some deep purple, some lime green, and some vibrant orange balls of wool.

"I'm sure your aunts will like those," she said.

I thanked her, and walked over to a white candle. "Do you have any incense?" I asked.

She shook her head. "They sell it at the shop at the other end of the street. They have incense, candles and gifts, and birthday cards, wrapping paper, you name it."

I thanked her and left the store. It was quite a shock to step out into a wall of heat after the icy air conditioning of the shop. I walked past several cafés, and I noticed one that I would like to return to at some point. It was only a stone's throw away from the water, not the surf, but the nearby river. It was a shame that no cafés I had yet seen were actually waterfront, but this was quite close enough and had a lovely view of the whale watching boats and the people on jet skis.

I turned and walked along the street in the direction of the gift store, and found it easily enough. It was dark inside, unlike the bright wool store. Still, it was more magical than gloomy. A huge diffuser pumped scented steam into the air. I identified cloves, cinnamon, lemon, and rosemary, as well as a hint of eucalyptus oil. It reminded me of Lucas.

I shook myself and headed straight for the incense. Dragons Blood, a red Indonesian resin, was one of my most favourite incenses in the world. I picked up a packet and inhaled deeply. I couldn't really afford any incense at this time, but I thought it would be good to know where everything was so that when I got my first pay from my aunts I could come here and stock up on my witch supplies. The store had all my favourite types of incense. Apart from Dragons Blood, there was frankincense, myrrh, white sage, vanilla, Nag Champa, lemongrass, rose musk, and ylang ylang.

The candles smelt delightful, too. I noted that the prices were reasonable, and I was pleased to see a good range of colours. I liked to use green candles for money drawing spells, purple candles for protection, orange candles for removing obstacles, and pink candles for romance. I hadn't used any pink candles lately—I had just about given up on that score.

That was when I saw the silver-framed photograph, exactly the same one I had seen in Lucas's cottage. In fact, they had an array of them, in all different shapes and sizes. When I saw the person in them, I gasped. It was the woman with the long blonde hair standing on a beach, her hair blowing in the wind. Not only was it the same woman, it was the identical photograph. And what's more, the very same photograph was in every single frame and every single size on display.

What were the chances that Lucas actually knew this woman? Could she be a famous model? No, that was too far fetched. I dismissed that idea quickly. Lucas had made sure I had seen that photograph and had tried to tell me it was someone he knew well.

"Can I help you?" The tone was friendly. I turned to look into the face of one of the two shop assistants, who hadn't bothered to speak to me until now. Both had been texting on their phones.

"I was shocked to see this photo," I said. "I saw it at someone's house the other day, and I thought it must be his girlfriend. I had no idea it was just a common photo in a frame."

The woman shrugged. "We never sell any of those," she said. "We sell lots of incense and candles, and those dreamcatchers over there." She pointed to an array of beautiful dreamcatchers hanging on the nearby wall. "These frames are half price right now."

"I'm really not interested in those frames," I said, "but I'll be back in a week or so to buy incense and candles."

"Are you sure? They're a bargain. We're selling at wholesale prices."

I shook my head. "Sorry, but I don't have any use for them."

She nodded. "Oh well, I've only sold one in the last few months. It was just the other day. We only had that one out on display, but after I sold it, we decided to put all the others out on display."

I made to turn away, but then I thought of

Lucas. "Did you sell it to a tall man, broad shoulders, a bit of stubble? Dark blue eyes?"

"Yes," she said. "I hadn't seen him before. He must be holidaying here. He was gorgeous." She said it with such feeling, I was surprised she didn't drool.

Lucas O'Callaghan had bought a photograph from the store and implied it was someone important to him. Why would he do such a thing? Did he truly think all women wanted to throw themselves at him? And this was his protection?

I decided to catch a taxi to Mugwort Manor at once. I had lost my appetite for window shopping. I was irritated, and I didn't know why. I just felt out of sorts.

After I paid the driver, I saw Lucas and Aunt Agnes in discussion. She was waving a pair of pruning shears. As I drew closer, I could hear them discussing hawthorn bushes.

"Did you enjoy your time in town?" Aunt Agnes asked me. "Next time you should take my car."

Lucas ignored me completely, picking a hawthorn berry from the branches and turning it over in his fingers.

"Yes, I did. I did some window shopping, too."

Still the disinterest from Lucas, but Agnes turned to me. "Where did you go?"

"I went to the wool shop and bought you and the other aunts a little gift, of wool, obviously," I said. "I do hope you like it."

Agnes clasped her hands in delight and pointed to the bag I was carrying. "Is it in there?"

I nodded and opened the bag so she could look inside. "Merino, my favourite!"

I could not resist baiting Lucas. "I saw some lovely silver-framed photographs in the gift shop, the one that sells the candles and the incense," I said to Aunt Agnes.

"That's a lovely shop," she said, but I wasn't looking at her, I was looking at Lucas. I saw his whole body tense.

I pushed on. "Yes, they had about fifty silver frames, all with the same photograph, a woman with her hair streaming out behind her and standing on a beach," I said. "She looked familiar. I'm sure I've seen that photo somewhere recently."

Lucas looked up at me then. His eyes burned into me, but I held his gaze. Aunt Agnes nodded absently and then walked along the flagstone pathway, snipping away at the hawthorn bushes with her pruning shears seemingly at random.

For the first time since I had met him, Lucas looked awkward. He shifted from one foot to the other. "About that photo…" he began, but I forestalled him.

"It's none of my business," I said. Still, I was curious, so I stood there, hoping he would enlighten me.

"Women often, err, come onto me," he said, "so I find it useful to have a photograph as a safeguard."

"Oh." It was the only polite reply I could muster. This guy really did have tabs on himself. "Well then, goodbye."

His expression showed that he was confused by my reaction, although I had no idea why. I left him standing there, staring after me, while I walked up the flagstone pathway, clutching my bag of Merino wool. My exit lost some of its effect when a huge bluetongue lizard ran across my path, stopped to hiss at me, and then disappeared into the bushes.

CHAPTER 16

I had only gone two steps when a police car screeched to a halt. I spun around to see Constable Walker jump out of the car and run over to Lucas. "Why isn't your phone turned on?"

"What's happened?" he asked her.

"We've been trying to call. There's been a fire at the winery. I have to attend a burglary call, or otherwise I'd give you a lift there." She was visibly disappointed that she couldn't, but nevertheless, she jumped back in her car and sped off.

"Pepper, could I borrow your phone to call a cab?" Lucas said.

I pointed to the silver Porsche. "Why don't you take your car?"

"I couldn't get it to start just then," he said, "and my phone's back in my cottage."

"Valkyrie will drive you in my Mazda," Aunt Agnes said, still brandishing the pruning shears.

"Can't he just borrow your car?" I asked her.

Aunt Agnes avoided my eyes. "You've put me in a difficult position with that question," she said. "You know I only allow family to drive that car."

I didn't know that at all, but I grasped the fact that she wanted me to go to the winery to snoop. "Okay then," I said. "Where are your car keys?"

She pulled them from her pocket and tossed them to me. I caught them with one hand, and then wished I hadn't done so, as the keys struck me on my knuckle.

I moved towards her car, and then realised that Lucas was standing stock still. I expected he wanted to have a say in whether or not I drove him to the winery. I supposed he thought I would try to put him in a compromising position. "Are you coming or not?" I said abruptly.

He hurried to the car by way of answer, and climbed into the passenger seat. "I don't know the way," I told him. "Well, I know the way as far as I got the other day when I had the flat tire, just past the turn off to the lighthouse."

"I'll direct you." His words were terse.

I shrugged. The man truly was unbearable. It was just such a pity he was gorgeous to look at. And then there was the chemistry. With that on my mind, I took a corner a little too fast and the car went sideways. I shot a glance at Lucas. He didn't say a word, so that was something in his credit. I wasn't partial to back seat drivers.

"Your distant cousin, the wine scientist, was murdered, and then there was an attempted robbery, and now the fire," I said. "Someone's obviously trying to put you out of business."

"It seems that way," he said, looking straight ahead.

"Linda Williams said she was heading out to your winery. I hope she's okay."

"Linda Williams?" He turned to look at me. "Why was she going there?"

I shrugged. "No idea. You saw us earlier in the coffee shop. She asked to join me, and then she said she was going to the winery. I figured she just wanted to get away from her insufferable husband."

"It's not open for guests at the moment."

I wondered if Lucas knew Linda had dated his uncle. "She probably doesn't know that. After all, she's been going there for years so she probably thought it was business as usual."

"Quite possibly."

Two bush turkeys ran out in front of the car, and I braked heavily. "Sorry about that."

Lucas muttered something.

"Okay, this is as far as I know my way. You'll have to direct me from here."

"Just keep going down this road and I'll tell you when to turn off."

I did as I was bid. "You know, I've been thinking, I don't think burglaries in town have anything to do with what's happening at your winery. No one else in town has been murdered or had cases of arson."

"I've reached the same conclusion," he said.

"No doubt that's what the police think, too."

Lucas pointed ahead. "Take the next turn to the left. See, just up there."

I slowed down. I took the turn, and drove down the road a short way. He didn't need to direct me any further; it was clear where I needed to go. Two fire trucks and two police vehicles were parked outside the closest large building.

I drove straight over to them, somewhat relieved that the fire didn't appear to have done much damage, at least not to the outside of the buildings.

Owen hurried over to us. "What are you doing here, Pepper?"

"Obviously I brought Lucas," I said.

"Was anyone hurt?" Lucas asked him.

"The managers are unharmed," Owen said. "They're inside showing an officer the damage, which doesn't seem to be severe, thanks to your good sprinkler system."

Lucas made to go to the building, but Owen caught his arm. I could tell Lucas didn't like being touched, because the tension in the air at once was palpable. "Before you go in, I need to speak to you about Linda Williams."

"Is she okay?" I asked him.

"She's missing. Her car's over there, but there's no sign of her." I followed his gaze to a black Audi parked under a tree.

"It's locked, and we found her handbag on the ground."

I gasped. "You don't think she started the fire?"

Owen shrugged. "If you're asking whether she started the fire and perished inside, no. The sprinkler system kept the damage to a minimum. When did you last see her?"

"I had coffee with her earlier," I said. "I was at a coffee shop today, and she came over and asked if she could join me. She said she was going to the winery later."

Owen looked at Lucas. "And you?"

"I was briefly in the café and saw the two of them talking, but then I left. That was the last time I saw Linda Williams."

Owen turned back to me. "How was she acting? Depressed?"

"I don't know her at all," I pointed out. "She seemed normal to me."

"Did she say why she was going out to the winery?"

I shook my head. "She did say she used to date Henry Ichor and she had a grudge against him. Apparently, he told her he didn't want to have a serious relationship, but she couldn't resist him. He also told her to buy shares. She said if she'd held them, they'd be worth a lot today, but she sold early. She blames him for that too, because she said he should've explained more fully. That doesn't make sense to me, but the thing is, she had a grudge against Henry Ichor." I looked at Lucas, but he didn't seem upset or surprised at my disclosure.

Owen nodded. "All right then, Pepper, I'll ask

you to drive back home now. This is a crime scene. One of the officers can take Mr O'Callaghan back when he's finished here."

I turned to leave, but Lucas touched my arm. "Thank you." With that, he marched after Owen into the closest building.

A flock of huge black cockatoos appeared from nowhere, flying low and uttering their weird, blood-curdling cry.

I walked back to my car slowly. How had Linda Williams simply vanished like that? What was her connection to the winery? The only one I knew was that she used to date Henry Ichor, but she hadn't seen him in years, or so she said.

CHAPTER 17

I arrived back at Mugwort Manor anxious to tell my aunts what I had learnt.

They were all sitting in the living room, knitting, looking as though butter wouldn't melt in their mouths. Aunt Dorothy was breathless. I figured they had been up to something and then assembled in the living room to put on a good front for me.

I narrowed my eyes. "What have you all been up to?"

"Nothing," they said in unison.

"Is there much damage at the winery?" Aunt Agnes asked.

"No, but Linda Williams is missing. Her car and

handbag are there, but there's no sign of her. Her handbag was found on the ground," I added.

"That explains why the detectives were at their cottage," Aunt Maude said. "They must've been speaking with Paul Williams." She abandoned her knitting to pour me a glass of wine.

I accepted it and sat in the striped armchair. "I went to a café as you suggested, and Linda Williams saw me and came over."

All three aunts stopped knitting. "What did she have to say for herself?" Aunt Agnes said.

"She said she used to date Henry Ichor." The aunts raised their eyebrows, and I pushed on. "She has some sort of bizarre grudge against him due to investment advice he gave her years ago."

"But that hardly matters, does it?" Aunt Agnes said. "We know he was overseas when he died."

"Maybe not," I said, "but don't they say innocent people don't have alibis? She said she was here in this country when he was killed, but something else interesting, she also thought he was murdered. Anyway, the main thing is she ate a rare steak and she gobbled it up."

My aunts all looked confused, yet they restarted their knitting. "I'm not sure what the steak has to do with anything," Aunt Agnes said.

"I thought she might be the Shifter," I said. "She certainly was eating a huge amount of red meat, and cooked rare at that. Why, it was practically raw. It turned my stomach."

"Oh, I see. Valkyrie thinks werewolves exhibit dog-like behaviour when they're in the human form," Dorothy said to the other two aunts.

I was puzzled. "Are you saying that's not the case? But what about Marius eating all those steak pizzas? You seemed interested in that."

Aunt Agnes's eyes darted from side to side, as they always did when she was trying to avoid something. "No, werewolves don't eat a lot of meat when in the human form," she said with a smirk, "any more than they don't sniff other people's posteriors, and run after the postman and bite his leg."

I narrowed my eyes. I hadn't been mistaken, surely—I knew they thought it strange that Marius had eaten five steak pizzas. They also seemed quite interested in what I had to say about Linda. Surely they were withholding information from me once more. "So are you saying she's not the Shifter?"

Aunt Agnes shook her head. "I'm not saying that at all. She could well be the Shifter. All I'm saying is, eating lots of red meat doesn't mean that someone is a Shifter. Yowies, that is, non-Shifter Yowies, are known to eat nuts and berries as well as killing for their food."

I bit my lip. "Oh well, I had better start work on your website."

Aunt Agnes stood up so fast I hardly saw her move. "I don't think you should sit in a stuffy house and work on the website until later," she said. "You haven't even been to the beach yet. Why don't you go to the beach now?"

I figured I might as well come out and ask. "Are you trying to get rid of me?"

"Oh no, no," all aunts said in unison, a guilty look travelling over each one's face.

I considered calling them on it, but then again, I hadn't been to the beach yet. "Okay then. I just don't want to let you down."

"Of course you're not letting us down, Valkyrie," Aunt Agnes said with a smile. "Go and have a nice walk along the beach. That will soothe your nerves, and when you get back, I'll have lunch waiting for you."

I thanked her and went to my bedroom to change into shorts and a top. I was looking forward to the beach. When I walked back down the stairs, all three aunts were sitting there primly, knitting. I suspected that if I returned after five minutes or so, I would catch them doing something—but what?

I said goodbye and left the house by the kitchen door. I had to walk past the cottages on my way to the beach, and I hoped I wouldn't come across Lucas O'Callaghan, who would no doubt think I was seeking him out.

I loved the smell of sea air, and took a deep breath as I made my way down the sandy path to the beach. It was nice to have direct access from the back of the Mugwort Manor estate. Lighthouse Bay had five beaches, four of them in town.

I stopped and sighed with sheer delight when I reached the edge of the beach. To my right was a viewing platform, and to my left and off in the distance, at the top of a sheer cliff, was the lighthouse.

I left my sandals alongside the sandy path on a clump of grass, and walked on barefoot. This was not a patrolled beach, at least not at this end. The patrolled beach was off to my right towards the lighthouse, and was where people went to swim and surf. Mugwort Manor backed onto the long dog beach, a designated off-leash dog area that stretched for a considerable distance until the next headland.

I passed an elderly couple with a white poodle

that was barking at a Great Dane, much to the consternation of the Great Dane's owner. I walked on, letting the waves lap at my feet. The tide was coming in, so I kept a close eye on the surf. I didn't want to walk too far, not with a Shifter on the loose, but my aunts had assured me that Shifters didn't kill randomly—that the murder had been a target on a particular person. Still, I thought it better to be prudent, and at any rate, I didn't want to walk too far up a lonely beach.

Still, I soon forgot myself and fell into a rhythm of walking through the gently lapping waves. It was so peaceful, listening to the seagulls and the rhythmic crashing of the waves, and revelling in the scent of the crisp salt air. The light breeze was gentle on my skin. Although it was summer, the temperature was entirely bearable.

The cry of a seagull broke me from my reverie, and I realised with a start that the beach was deserted—not a dog or an owner in sight.

My right eye twitched.

My heart beat faster and I broke into a cold sweat. I could feel the danger, almost taste it.

I turned around and picked up the pace, heading back to Mugwort Manor.

I saw movement ahead to my left, in the sand

dunes, all of which were covered with tea trees and tall scrubby undergrowth. I hoped it wasn't a Shifter. Much to my relief, I saw that the movement in the undergrowth was moving away from me and not towards me. The figure continued to move away from me, and my breathing calmed somewhat.

I could see a head, and could make out the shape of a man. Still, that didn't mean the man couldn't transform into a Shifter, but it would be rather a silly thing to do on a beach that was a popular off-leash dog beach.

I edged closer to the sand dunes and away from the water, but continued walking back to the Manor. The man now came to a standstill, so I hesitated. There was something in his hand. I thought it was a shovel, but I was too far away to see.

I kept walking, but I edged ever closer to the soft sand. He was still between me and the manor, but I thought it wouldn't hurt to look—although what if he chased me?

The thought of someone chasing me scared me, so I decided to walk back down to the water where the sand was firm, and I would be able to run if it came to that. Yet no sooner had I made the decision, than the man spotted me. I stopped and froze on the spot.

He waved to me in a friendly fashion, and I waved back. I thought it best to act like I hadn't caught him doing something wrong. In fact, I didn't know if I had, but what would someone be doing scuttling along in the undergrowth? No one ever walked up there.

The man headed towards me, and I didn't know what to do. Should I make a run for it? Or should I stand my ground and talk to him? If I acted like I didn't think he was doing anything wrong, I might be able to talk my way out of it, assuming he did have ill intent towards me. I was also taking it as a good sign that he hadn't transformed into a Shifter.

He was close now, and I could see it was Marius Jones. I did my best to calm my breathing as he approached me.

"Hello Pepper, enjoying a walk?"

"Yes, I am."

"I just saw a dog running into the bushes, so I went after him," Marius said.

I thought he was lying, but of course I had to go along with it. "So you didn't catch him?" I said.

"No, he was much too fast for me. I'm

concerned because I can't see any owners around looking for a dog."

"Did he have a collar?" I asked him, playing along with his story. I did, however, notice he was covered in dog hair.

"Yes, a red one," Marius said after hesitating for some time. "I couldn't get close enough to catch him."

"I wouldn't worry," I said. "There are no roads out this way, so it's not as if he'll run into traffic. He'll probably find his way home, or the owners will come this way looking for him. You could call the council and the local vet and report what you saw."

"Thanks, Pepper. That's a good idea."

I had to fight the urge to run, because my right eye was twitching madly and I knew something was wrong.

Marius took a step towards me and I involuntarily took a step backwards. "So you didn't see a dog?"

I shook my head. "I wasn't looking for a dog, though. I was off in my own world, enjoying my walk."

"But you saw me," Marius pointed out.

"That's true."

"What exactly did you see?" His manner had become threatening, not overly so, but his voice held a clear undertone of menace.

"Just you looking for the dog," I said in my best imitation of a nonchalant manner.

"You shouldn't be out walking by yourself, Pepper," he said, his eyes flashing angrily. "There has already been *one* murder."

I measured the distance between us, and the distance to the sandy path that led to the manor. I didn't think I would be able to sprint away from him. Also, if I ran, then he would know I didn't trust him, and I didn't know if the situation had deteriorated quite to that degree.

"Pepper!"

I could have cried with relief. Lucas was striding up the beach towards us. I noticed that Marius took a step backwards and faced him.

"What are you doing here?" Lucas asked me in an abrupt manner.

"Going for a walk along the beach, of course," I snapped. For all I knew, he had just saved my life, but his unpleasant, superior manner still rankled.

"I'm sorry to intrude. Were the two of you out for a walk together?" Lucas addressed the question to Marius.

"Not at all. I was out walking by myself and saw a stray dog, so I went looking for him," Marius said.

"And I saw Marius looking for the dog in the bushes, so he came over to speak to me," I said, and then wondered why I had explained it at all.

"Pepper, I'll walk you back. I assume you're going to keep looking for the dog, Marius?"

Marius said that he was. He left us and walked along the sand. Dark waves of anger were still emanating from him.

Lucas watched him go, and then turned to me. "Did he threaten you?"

I shrugged. "I'm not entirely sure, but I did feel that I was in danger. I saw him doing something in the bushes. He walked from that direction, back over there." I pointed to where I had first seen Marius. "I was watching him for some time, and then he saw me and came over."

"You didn't think that was a dangerous thing to do? There *is* a murderer on the loose, you know."

"I'm aware of that, and for all I know, it could be you." I regretted the words as soon as they were out of my mouth.

Lucas looked at me appraisingly, while biting his lip. "Yes, that's right. You shouldn't trust anyone at this point, only your aunts. Having said that, please allow me to escort you back to them."

"Aren't you afraid that I'll throw you to the ground and have my wicked way with you?" I had no idea why I said that, either. Perhaps it was the relief that I was now in no danger from Marius, if I ever had been in the first place, but there was something off about the man. And besides, my eye did not twitch when I was around Lucas.

Lucas did not respond, and that made me feel even more foolish. "We should walk on the hard sand," he said, and I agreed, following him back down to the water.

"The beach is my favourite place in the world," he said.

I was so surprised that he was making conversation that I didn't speak for a minute. "Mine, too. If I do in fact end up staying with my aunts, I'm going to get a dog."

"Why don't you have a dog now?" he asked me.

"Because I couldn't afford one," I said, standing still for a moment as a big wave sent some deeper water towards us. "I believe that if someone has a dog, then that person has to be able to afford vet care, and everything like that."

"Quite so." We fell into silence after that, but it

was a pleasant silence. I thought how the waitresses had fawned all over him, and how Linda Williams had said he was attractive. He certainly *was* attractive. I shook my head to clear it. I shouldn't be having these thoughts, especially not with him walking beside me.

"My aunts said that your wine was a special wine, full of vitamins and minerals," I said.

To my surprise, Lucas stopped, and swung me to him. "What did you just say?" His tone was urgent, his touch light but imperative.

I was taken aback. "I just said that my aunts mentioned that your wine, you know, the wine from the Ambrosia Winery, was full of vitamins and minerals."

He released me, but I could still feel the tingles coursing through my body at his touch. Why did he react like that? I had at first thought he'd misheard me, but he had appeared just as worried when I repeated it.

We walked back to the manor in silence, but not a companionable silence now. It was decidedly frosty.

CHAPTER 18

I expected that Lucas would go into his cottage as we walked past it, but he continued on with me to the manor itself. I didn't know why, but it was obvious that he was tense.

I opened the kitchen door for him and he walked inside. My aunts were sitting at the kitchen table, knitting. It was almost as if they expected him.

"Sorry to intrude, ladies," he said, "but Pepper here just mentioned something interesting about my wine, and I thought I'd ask you."

Aunt Agnes raised one eyebrow, but the other aunts' expressions remained impassive. "Yes, we'd be glad to help if we can," she said.

I noticed she didn't offer him some coffee, or

anything like that. They were acting normal, knitting away, but I knew they were tense.

"I don't know much about the Ambrosia Winery," Lucas said, "and I'm hoping to learn more, obviously. It's just that Pepper mentioned something that my managers have never mentioned to me. She said you told her that the wine was special, full of vitamins and minerals."

Aunt Agnes did not miss a beat. "Yes of course. Didn't you know that? It's a very special wine, full of all sorts of good things. It's low in alcohol and not like other wine."

I could feel Lucas's tension growing. "How do you know that?"

"Well, your uncle told us, of course," she said. The other two aunts continued to knit, more furiously than ever.

Lucas crossed his arms over his chest. "I thought you said you didn't know him well?"

"He wasn't a close friend or anything like that," Aunt Agnes said, "but everyone knows everyone else in a small town like this. Plus years ago we used to serve dinner to the guests and we used his wine then. He used to sell it to us at a good discount. He said it was more like a special herbal wine. Don't tell me he was wrong?" She widened her eyes, a picture of innocence.

I could feel Lucas relaxing beside me. "Thank you," he said.

"Does that help?" Agnes asked him.

He nodded. "Yes, I think so. It's a shame the managers didn't tell me that. I hope all Henry's secrets didn't die with him."

My hand flew to my mouth. "Surely not?"

Lucas turned to face me. "What do you mean?"

"If your uncle Henry had a secret formula, then obviously your cousin, the wine scientist knew it, too. Now both your uncle and the wine scientist are dead. Do you think someone was after the secret formula to your wine?"

"Yes, I suppose that's possible," Lucas said slowly, tapping his chin, "but it's not as if it's a famous winery or anything like that. Who would care about wine from my winery? Uncle Henry never entered any wine shows or competitions. The winery mainly flies under the radar. I doubt anyone would kill somebody just to discover my uncle's methods."

"Well, I think you should consider the possibility," I said flatly. "If it was full of vitamins and minerals, like your uncle said, then..." My voice trailed away. I wasn't sure where I was going with that train of thought. "Your uncle died, and I don't know if he was murdered, but we know for a fact that the wine scientist was murdered, and I think that's too much of a coincidence."

Lucas nodded. "You could well be right. Anyway, sorry to intrude, ladies." With that, he nodded and let himself out.

I turned to my aunts who at once let out a collective sigh of relief. "What was that about?" I asked them.

"That's a conversation for another time," Aunt Agnes said. "Meanwhile, it's best if you never mention anything we say to you about his wine to Mr O'Callaghan."

"Whyever not?"

No one answered, so I said, "Let me guess. That's a conversation for another time, right? Anyway, I haven't told you what just happened to me."

All sets of knitting needles stopped.

"I was walking along the beach, when I saw Marius Jones off in the scrub, acting suspiciously."

"Acting suspiciously, how?" Aunt Agnes asked me.

"He might have been burying something, but I

can't be sure," I said, "and then he saw me. I think he threatened me."

"You *think* he threatened you?" Agnes said, parroting me once more.

"Not with his words as such, but certainly his manner," I said. "I thought he had a shovel, but I was too far away. He didn't seem happy when he realised I had seen him. Now, what's all this secrecy about the wine from Ambrosia Winery?"

"It's Witches' Brew," Aunt Agnes said, and the other two aunts nodded furiously.

"Lucas O'Callaghan's uncle Henry was a witch?"

Agnes shrugged. "Yes, and um…" She hesitated for a moment, and then said, "He made the Witches' Brew. The beauty of it is that ordinary, non-witch people can drink it, but when witches do, it enhances our powers."

I sat down on the nearest chair and clutched my head. "This is all too much."

"You've seen that Yowie Shifter, right?" Aunt Dorothy reminded me.

"Yes," I said slowly.

"Your mind should now be more open to the paranormal," Aunt Agnes said with a hint of censure in her voice.

I sighed. "It is, but there's a limit."

"Never mind, Valkyrie, I've made you your favourite lunch," Aunt Agnes said. "Macaroni cheese."

I thanked her politely. I detested macaroni cheese. Years earlier, when visiting with my parents, the aunts had served us macaroni cheese. I had said it was nice, simply to be polite, and ever since then, Aunt Agnes had it in her head that it was my favourite food and served it up to me at every opportunity.

I warily eyed the huge plate of macaroni cheese that Aunt Agnes deposited in front of me. "And have some wine with that," she said, fetching the crystal goblet seemingly out of thin air, and filling it.

"The Witches' Brew," I said.

"Yes, but you don't want to call it that in front of other people."

I nodded. I realised I had already said too much in front of Lucas O'Callaghan.

The aunts only picked at their food, and I noticed they were all looking at me. By the time I had finished my meal, I not only felt somewhat sick to my stomach, but I also felt somewhat apprehensive.

"Now Valkyrie, I have something to tell you."

My stomach clenched, and I instinctively took a large gulp of the Witches' Brew.

"What is it this time?" I said. "There are fairies at the bottom of the garden?"

"Would you be surprised if there were?" Aunt Maude said.

I gasped, but Aunt Agnes waved her hand at Maude. "Not as far as we know, but nothing would surprise me, Valkyrie. Now, we've been discussing how to break this to you gently, and you seeing the Yowie Shifter was a good start."

I took another gulp of wine. "You're saying that the Yowie Shifter was just a start?" I was incredulous.

All the aunts nodded solemnly. "Now, this might upset you a little, Valkyrie."

"Will it be more upsetting than finding out that Shifters are real?" I asked her.

The aunts exchanged glances. "Quite possibly," Agnes said, while Aunt Dorothy nodded frantically.

"Please just spit it out and get it over with then," I said. The apprehension was gnawing away at the pit of my stomach, a stomach already filled with rich macaroni cheese.

"We are vampires."

The wine had been halfway to my mouth, but

when she said that, I set my goblet down hard on the table. "Please tell me this is a joke," I said weakly.

"No, all three of us are vampires," Agnes said.

I clutched my throat. "You drink blood?"

The three of them looked horrified. "Oh goodness me, no! That's so last century, dear," Aunt Agnes said.

Aunt Dorothy shook her head. "Hollywood has a lot to answer for."

Aunt Maude agreed. "Drinking blood is so 1695."

"You don't kill people?" I asked hopefully.

Agnes gasped. "Of course not, dear."

"But what do you do for, you know, blood? Do you drink pigs' blood?"

"Why would we murder an innocent pig?" Aunt Agnes appeared to be shocked. "We're animal lovers. How could you say such a thing, Valkyrie?"

"Well, she obviously doesn't know anything about vampires, Agnes," Aunt Maude said harshly. "You had better explain it all to her."

Agnes snorted rudely. "How do I know what to explain? I don't know what she knows and what she doesn't know."

Aunt Dorothy piped up. "Obviously she knows nothing at all, zero, zilch, nil, nought, nothing."

"We're just like anyone else really," Aunt Agnes said, her eyes darting wildly from side to side. She wrung her hands. "We need a lot of iron, and that probably gave rise to the old myth of vampires drinking blood. Of course, for all we know they *did* drink blood, back in the day. Modern vampires need to take iron supplements, specifically, ferritin supplements. Just as vegans need to take Vitamin B12 daily, vampires need iron and certain other vitamins and minerals daily. That's about it."

"You forgot the bit about living for a long time," Aunt Maude prompted.

"How long?" It was too much of a shock to take in. The room receded slightly and I slurped some more wine. That seemed to steady me, but I set down my goblet and gripped the edges of my chair.

"Quite a long, long time," Aunt Agnes said in a nonchalant tone.

"Are you immortal?" I asked her. The room was now spinning.

"Of course not, dear." Agnes twisted her knitting needles nervously.

"Well, that's a relief," I said, looking at my aunts with new eyes.

"We would probably die if a bus ran over us," she pointed out.

"Or if we fell off a cliff," Maude said.

"Or if someone ran us through with a pitchfork," Dorothy added. "We might possibly die then. So you see, dear, we're not immortal."

I rubbed my temples and then looked up to see my aunts looking worriedly at each other.

"So how old are you exactly?" I asked them. "Hundreds of years old?"

"A lady never tells her age," Aunt Agnes said primly.

My curiosity overcame my fear, but it was all so surreal. "A little hint? Are you over one hundred years old? How old were you when you were turned?"

"Turned?" Aunt Dorothy said in confusion. "What's that?"

"You know, how you became vampires. Didn't someone bite your neck and you turned into a vampire?"

A look of disgust swamped Aunt Agnes's face. "There are so many horrible stories out there about vampires. It's not very nice. No, we were born this way. If you promise not to scream or faint, we'll show you our true form."

I gasped. Would they look like savage beasts? Before I could ask them not to show me their true form, the air around them shimmered.

There in front of me, were three strikingly beautiful women, all youthful, I guessed somewhere in their thirties. As I continued to stare, the air shimmered and once more they turned back into elderly ladies.

"We deliberately hide our true form, using this magical glamour," Aunt Agnes explained.

"Why, why?" I stammered.

Dorothy frowned at me. "So men won't hit on us, of course. Isn't that obvious?"

I had no reply.

"Yes, we can make ourselves look any age we like," Aunt Agnes said as if she were explaining something logical like photosynthesis or the law of relativity. "Most people tend to overlook and underestimate elderly ladies. They don't think we have minds of our own, and they tend to condescend to us. It's safer to be in this form."

"Tell her about the Witches' Brew," Maude said.

Aunt Agnes's eyes lit up. "Oh yes, the Witches' Brew. That is truly how we refer to it, but it's actually an elixir for vampires. Henry Ichor was a vampire and he produced this wine. He exported it to vampires worldwide. I'll explain it all more fully, when you're over this shock, Valkyrie, but Henry was both a witch and a vampire, both hereditary traits. For centuries, his bloodline has had the ability to produce the Witches' Brew. It's an innate ability, one his wine scientist relative had, too. The trouble is, there's no formula for Witches' Brew, so you can see it's quite a serious matter that both Henry and Talos Sparks are dead. Not all vampire-witches can make Witches' Brew, only those with the ability inherent in their bloodline. Only a vampire-witch, someone with the genes of both, can produce Witches' Brew, which refers more to the producer than the drinker."

The other two aunts nodded.

"So it's not for witches?" I asked. I wanted to ask more, but it was too much for me to handle.

"No, it's for vampires. I just explained that," Aunt Agnes said. "You're taking this quite well, Valkyrie."

"I'm really not," I said. "I think I'm going into shock."

"She's gone white," Dorothy said. "I hope she doesn't faint again. Agnes, you'd better not tell her that other thing yet."

Both Agnes and Maude rounded on her and shushed her, but it was too late.

I took another gulp of wine, dismayed to see the goblet was now empty, and asked, "What other thing?"

All the aunts looked concerned. I wondered what the other thing could possibly be. And that was when I began to put two and two together. The Witches' Brew was for vampires. They had been keen to have me drink plenty of the Witches' Brew. Vampires were born, not turned—it was genetic. I was their niece, perhaps their great-great-great-great-great grand niece, but the important thing was that I was their blood relative.

That was the last thing I remembered.

I came to on the floor, all three aunts bending over me, patting my hands.

Aunt Agnes tried to pour some wine into my mouth, but it went down the wrong way and I choked. I coughed and propped myself up on one elbow. I opened one eye. "I'm a vampire, aren't I?"

CHAPTER 19

I opened the other eye and tried to remember where I was. Oh yes, I was on the kitchen floor at Mugwort Manor, and my vampire aunts were bending over me. If I hadn't been lying down, no doubt I would have fainted again.

"Is Lucas a vampire, too?" I asked them.

"I don't think so, dear," Aunt Agnes said, brushing the remainder of the macaroni cheese off my clothes. I must have pulled the plate on top of me when I fainted.

"How do you know he isn't a Shifter, then?" I didn't resist when the aunts helped me back onto my chair. Aunt Dorothy poured me a glass of wine, and I took a large mouthful. "Are you sure this is low in alcohol?"

"One question at a time, Valkyrie," Aunt Agnes said sternly but not unkindly. "We don't know if Lucas O'Callaghan is a vampire, but we know for certain that he is not a Shifter. And the reason for that is that his uncle Henry was a vampire, and no vampire would have a Shifter as a relative."

"Why?" I was curious, in spite of myself.

"I can give you a long summary of the history later," Agnes said, "but suffice to say, vampires and Shifters have always been at each other's throats."

"Is that a pun?" I asked her. "Because if it is, I don't find it funny. I hope you understand that I've had a terrible shock, in fact, a few days of terrible shocks. So are you saying that you don't know if Lucas is a vampire, but he can't be a werewolf or any sort of Shifter, because his uncle was a vampire?"

All the aunts nodded happily. "She understands," Dorothy said triumphantly.

"No, I really don't," I said. I was on the verge of tears. In fact, I wanted to burst into deep sobs, and I was only barely managing to hold it together. "If I am a vampire because you're all vampires, then why isn't Lucas a vampire if his uncle was a vampire?"

"It's just like anything else that is passed down in families," Agnes said long-sufferingly, "quite like red hair, for example. It's just a question of genetics. Two parents with blue eyes will always produce a child with blue eyes, but two parents with brown eyes could also produce a child with blue eyes. Genetics!"

"Could I please have some Advil?"

The packet of Advil appeared in front of me as if by magic, along with a glass of water. "How did you move so fast?" I asked Aunt Dorothy.

"It's just an ability that I developed around a hundred years or so ago," she said calmly. "Now take two and soon you'll be feeling a lot better."

"I doubt it," I muttered darkly. "Let me see if I've got this right. Having vampire parents doesn't necessarily make the child a vampire?"

Aunt Agnes sighed. "Yes, having two vampire parents will make a child a vampire, but if a child has one vampire parent and one non-vampire parent, then the child has a fifty percent chance of being either. Didn't you do biology at school?"

"Yes, but it was all about pea plants and nothing about vampires," I said icily. "So you don't know if Lucas's parents were both vampires, is that right?"

"Quite so," Aunt Agnes said, "but both your

parents were vampires."

I put my head in my hands and rubbed my temples, staring hard at the yellowed lace doily under my plate, and tried to process the fact that both my parents were vampires. "Is there something you're not telling me?"

Aunt Agnes took a while to respond. "No dear, I'm sorry to say that we don't know what happened to your parents, if that's what you're thinking. But I *can* tell you that they were both vampires, and that's how we know that you're a vampire. And yes, as I mentioned just then, there has long been hatred between vampires and Shifters. It goes back a very long way. Don't try to understand now, but just remember that a Shifter is never your friend."

I thought that a rather strange piece of advice, but I filed it away for future reference. "So what happens now?"

"You eat your dessert, and then we'll keep up our work making this Yowie Shifter tell us who his accomplice is," Aunt Agnes said, as if she were talking about something as mundane as the weather forecast. "Simple, really."

Dorothy deposited a large bowl of chocolate ice cream in front of me. I thanked her and ate a spoonful before speaking. "I suspect Marius. He has a terrible temper, and I'm sure he made me a veiled threat."

Agnes nodded. "It could well be."

"Should we search his cottage?" I asked them. "I assume you have a master key?"

They all nodded. "But that won't be any help at all," Aunt Maude said. "Shifters wouldn't be careless enough to have evidence lying around about their homes."

I looked at the floor. Some macaroni cheese was still lying on it. "I'd better clean that up," I said.

Aunt Agnes stood up. "Nonsense. You go and lie on the couch and watch TV. We'll clean it up."

"I want to help," I protested weakly, but they wouldn't listen to me.

Soon I was lying on the big comfortable couch in the living room, watching TV, and clutching the remote. This wasn't how I imagined my life would play out. Suddenly I thought of fangs. Fangs! Why hadn't the aunts mentioned fangs? And I had been to many dentists, so why hadn't any of them said there was something strange about my teeth? I didn't have the energy to get up and ask them, so I just lay there and flipped through the channels, trying to find something to watch.

The black cat appeared from nowhere and

jumped up next to me on the couch. "I'm sorry, but I don't think there's an episode of *Gilmore Girls* on right now," I said in apology. The cat looked at me. "It's a toss up between *Antiques Roadshow* and *Love It or List It Vancouver*." The cat jumped off the couch and sat in front of the TV. She purred loudly and flicked her tail when I flicked the channel to *Love It or List It Vancouver*.

I lay back on the couch and tried to process the information. I had so many questions, apart from the fangs. And why had my parents tried to keep me away from my aunts? Was there something, even now, that my aunts weren't telling me?

And was I in danger from the other murderer, the accomplice of the creature locked in a magical cage in the room upstairs? Once again, I could feel hysteria bubbling away within me, and I fought against it. This was crazy, but at the same time, I knew it was real. I thought I needed to see a therapist, only I would be locked up in double quick time. I wondered if there was a therapist for vampires. I'd have to ask my aunts about that.

All three aunts came into the room just when the Vancouver house owners were about to announce whether they would love it or list it. "We're going for our afternoon walk now, Valkyrie,"

Aunt Agnes said. "We haven't been on our walk for a few days, and we have to keep healthy."

"Before you go, I have a question about fangs."

"Oh yes, fangs," Aunt Agnes said in a matter of fact manner. "That's not a very nice term, is it? They're just like wisdom teeth." She turned to leave.

"Wait a minute," I said. "What do you mean that they're like wisdom teeth?"

"They're not really like wisdom teeth," Aunt Maude said. "Some people never get their wisdom teeth, but vampires always get their fangs."

"Quite right," Agnes said. "You're probably too young to get your fangs yet, but don't be alarmed when you do. It doesn't hurt."

"Valkyrie is plenty old enough to have fangs now," Aunt Maude said. "She just has to learn how to use them."

"All right then. We'll talk about it later." Aunt Agnes addressed the comment to me. "Now you have a good sleep, Valkyrie. You've been through a lot and it must be a terrible strain on you. Have a nice sleep. The cat will keep you company."

The cat meowed in response.

I must have drifted off into a deep sleep. At some point, I remembered waking up and turning off the TV, but the rest was hazy. I dreamt I heard someone ringing the doorbell. I woke up, wondering if it had been a dream, but no one was ringing it any more, so I went back to sleep. When I woke up again, the cat wasn't there.

I sat up gingerly, feeling that awful yet fleeting sick feeling one gets when waking up suddenly from a deep sleep. I couldn't see anything around that had been responsible for waking me. I yawned and stretched and then winced at the pain in my neck. I had been lying at a funny angle on the couch. Still, I felt more relaxed than I had in a while.

And then it all came flooding back to me. I was a vampire.

I touched my hand to my mouth and felt along my teeth. There was not a single pointy one there. I wished the aunts had explained about fangs before they'd left. Still, as modern day vampires apparently didn't bite anyone, I supposed they didn't need big, unwieldy fangs. I hoped so, anyway.

And something else occurred to me in my newly awakened state. If I were to have a long-term boyfriend, he would have to be a vampire too, or I would outlive him. This wasn't good. It was hard enough finding a suitable man. Gosh, I hadn't even managed to do that yet, and now I had to find a suitable man who was also a vampire. What were the chances of that?

I threw up my hands in horror. My life was rapidly going downhill. Here I was, a vampire living with my elderly vampire aunts who weren't really elderly but wanted to look that way, at a Bed and Breakfast that didn't actually serve breakfast, but had bizarrely themed cottages. And then there was the Yowie Shifter locked upstairs in the magical cage. I lay back down and rubbed my throbbing temples.

Just as I did so, I heard a noise directly above me in the bedroom. I could tell it was from my newly improved hearing, which I figured was a result of the Witches' Brew. I sensed it wasn't the aunts. Was it the Yowie Shifter? Had he escaped? I trembled with fear.

I held my breath and listened again, but this person, if it was a person, was moving around quietly. I imagined that if the Shifter had escaped, he would hightail it to freedom rather than go on a tour of the house.

With that thought boosting what little courage I had, I quietly walked in the direction of the stairs. I sneaked up the stairs, alarmed that most of them creaked under my weight, and then headed in the direction of the aunts' bedroom wing. When I reached Aunt Agnes's door, I saw a man inside.

I ducked back, and tried to catch my breath. I wiped my sweaty palms on my jeans and did the breathing exercises, as best I could.

I risked another glance and to my shock, it was Marius. He was looking through the drawers and shoving jewellery in bags. He was the burglar!

What was I to do? I was unarmed, and I didn't know if he was. What's more, I didn't know if he was a Shifter, but if he was, I figured he would have already released his accomplice. No, this was a burglary, plain and simple.

Still, that didn't mean I wouldn't be in danger from him, if he were to discover me. I backtracked until I came to a fork in the hallway and I ducked down it. I had entered the sergeant's number into my phone, and I at once sent him a text, after being careful to turn off the sound on the phone first. I would be discovered for sure if my phone rang right now.

I texted Owen and told him that Marius Jones was currently robbing the house and I was hiding in the house. The text was at once marked as delivered, but I didn't know if he had actually read it. I decided to give him a few moments and then I would call. With that in mind, I edged further away from Marius so he wouldn't hear me if I had to make a call.

I hadn't got far before Owen texted me back. He told me to hide and that the police would be there any minute.

Then I had a horrible thought. What if Owen came upstairs and found the room with the Shifter? Should I try to draw Marius downstairs before Owen got there? I was at a loss as to what to do.

Just then, I heard Marius coming my way. I hoped he would go straight back down the staircase and not in the direction of the Shifter. Another horrible thought occurred to me. What if Marius heard the police coming and ran for cover down to the room with the Shifter?

There was nothing else for it. I had to prevent that at all costs. I took off at a fast pace and ran to the corridor, and stood there, blocking the way to the room.

I didn't know what I would do if Marius came my way, but I hoped that my fangs would somehow appear in the case of emergency.

I heard the police siren then. It sounded far away, yet moments later, it seemed much closer. I heard Marius's footsteps heading my way at speed.

Before he reached me, I heard the front door fly open, and someone yell, "Police!"

It was just as I feared. Marius ran from the police straight down to the forbidden corridor. When he saw me, he stopped in his tracks. I bared my teeth at him, willing my fangs to pop out. Nothing happened.

I must have scared him at any rate, as he turned and ran in the opposite direction. I breathed a sigh of relief. I ran down the corridor to see Owen launching himself on top of Marius, and after a brief struggle, Owen handcuffed his arms behind his back. "Take him away," he said to two uniformed officers. "Pepper, are you all right?"

I realised I was shaking. "I'm not really all right," I said. "I've never been so scared."

"Well, it's all over now," Owen said brightly. "Good work, Pepper. You caught the burglar."

"You're the one who actually caught him," I said with a laugh, relief flooding through me now that Marius was being dragged out the front door in handcuffs by the two uniformed officers. My right eye twitched, but the danger was now over. Marius was the burglar and most likely the Yowie Shifter, too. He simply must not have realised that my aunts were the ones who captured the other Shifter.

CHAPTER 20

Outside the front door, two uniformed officers hurried up to us. "There's nothing in his cottage, no sign of any stolen goods," one said.

Owen muttered something rude.

"I think I know where he might have hidden them," I said excitedly, after the officers left. "I saw him at the beach earlier today, and I thought he had a shovel. He seemed quite annoyed that I'd seen him and he kind of threatened me."

Owen took a step towards me. "He threatened you? Why didn't you tell me?"

"Well, it was a veiled threat more than anything explicit as such," I said. "But if Mr O'Callaghan hadn't been walking along the beach at the time, goodness knows what would have happened."

Owen visibly bristled when I mentioned Lucas's name. "So where did you see this happen?"

"Sorry, I should've started from the beginning. I was walking along the off-leash dog beach, and I saw someone off in the scrub. He was bending over, and I was quite sure I saw a shovel. He saw me looking at him and came over."

"Was he holding a shovel then?"

"He wasn't holding anything at all."

Owen frowned. "And you didn't see a shovel or anything? He wasn't holding anything?"

I shook my head. "No, nothing."

"Do you think you'd be able to find that same spot again?"

"I don't know, it's hard. One section of beach looks the same as the other, but I might be able to find it. It was just past the submerged rock in the water, and just past a clump of tea trees." I thought some more. "Yes, I'd probably be able to find it."

"Can you take me there now?" Owen asked.

"Sure."

Owen called to the officers who were putting Marius in the car. "Be very, very careful with him. He could be a lot more dangerous than he looks.

Don't take any chances; he could possibly be the murderer. And if so, he's very strong, even stronger than he looks. Don't take any chances," he said once more.

The officers acknowledged his words and drove away. "I'll have to leave a note for my aunts," I said. I made to go back to the house, but Owen touched my arm.

"Here you go, write it on this." He handed me his notepad and paper.

I scrawled a quick note, telling the aunts about Marius, and that I was showing Owen where I had last seen Marius on the beach. Owen took the notepad from me and ripped out the sheet. "Be right back," he said, and then he ran up the flagstone path.

We didn't pass anyone on the way to the beach, and the off-leash dog beach was deserted. This was likely due to the heat. Most people came out early morning or late afternoon in this type of weather.

We walked along the beach making small talk, until I saw the rock. "See that rock there?" I pointed to it and waved my hands at the small rocks around it. "I saw him just past that rock, and see that line of tea trees there, all that scrub? It was just past there."

Owen and I left the hard, wet sand and walked over to the soft sand at the high section of the beach. It was quite difficult to walk through. I stopped when we came to the sand dunes covered with spinifex grass.

"Now take your time, Pepper," Owen said. "Think it through. This could be quite important."

I nodded. I walked around, trying to think where I had seen Marius. "I'm sorry Owen, I thought it was around here, but I just can't see anything."

"Are you sure it was around here?"

"Yes, it was definitely here. I had just passed that rock, and he was just past the line of tea trees, but it all looks different from this angle."

"Like I said, I've just moved to the area," Owen said, "so are there any buildings around here like isolated old beach shacks, somewhere anyone could hide stolen goods?"

I shrugged. "I haven't been here for years, but I don't think there's anything like that at all. I suppose those trees could be hiding something, but I saw him out here in the open."

Owen stroked his chin. "Stay here and have a look around, but don't wander off. I don't want to have to go searching for you as well as the stolen goods. I'll just go behind those trees and see if there's a beach shack hidden there."

After Owen left in the direction of the tea trees, I skirted around the scrub. Of course, it would be impossible to see if anyone had walked this way, given that it was sandy, so any tracks would be hidden. I couldn't see anything at all. I walked around in circles, keeping my eyes on the last clump of tea trees as a point of reference.

I looked up; Owen was certainly taking his time. I wondered if he had found something. I turned my attention back to the ground and made yet another circle, and that's when I saw it. The shovel.

It was lying flat on the ground, but I could see an area next to it that had recently been dug up. I dropped to my knees and felt around with my hands for a bit. I uncovered what looked like a canvas bag close to the surface. The stolen goods!

I stood up. "Owen, I found it!" I called out as loudly as I could in the direction of the trees.

I looked back down at the sand. There was a large area that had recently been dug up. It seemed to me it was sufficiently large to stash a considerable amount of loot, and the ground was quite soft. It had been clever of Marius. No one ever walked this way—people walked their dogs along the beach and didn't venture across into the sand dunes. They led nowhere and were largely impassable.

Where was Owen? I cupped my hands around my mouth, and called again. "Owen, I found it!"

Then it dawned on me. The man my aunts held captive should be considered missing, as far as the townspeople knew, but there had been no report of a missing person. The only person who appeared to be absent was Ethan Carteron.

I turned around to flee. I saw a flash of brown, and then I saw it, right next to my bare leg. It was an Eastern Brown snake, the second most deadly snake in the whole world, a big one, longer than the shovel next to it. I could see its underbelly, the distinctive orange-pink markings. In a flash, I realised I could see those markings because it was striking at me.

The next thing I knew, I was standing on the other side of the clearing. I gasped. This speed must be a latent vampire power that had been helped along by the Witches' Brew. I had seen my aunts move swiftly like this, but I hadn't imagined that I myself would be able to do it. And just as well, too. I didn't know if snakes could kill vampires, but I figured a bite from a deadly snake wouldn't do me any good.

I turned around, and there, only inches from my eyes, was a huge hairy chest. I looked up into the face of a Yowie.

The next thing I remembered was waking up in a dark room. I had a moment of blind panic, thinking I was in a coffin. I lifted my hands above my head, and to my relief, I didn't touch anything. I felt along the wall beside me. It seemed to be brick, and was damp. The unmistakeable scent of mould hung in the air and tickled my nose.

I felt the floor and realised it was concrete. I pulled myself to my feet, and peered into the surrounding gloom.

What had happened to me?

My head was so sore that I figured the Yowie had hit me over the head with something, probably his meaty fist. Tentatively, I felt my scalp, and there was a sizeable lump. It felt ghastly, all spongy, and was painful to touch.

The Yowie had obviously brought me here, but for what purpose? What did it intend to do with me? Had it hurt Owen, or was he the Yowie?

Still, there was no time to feel sorry for myself; I had to find a way of escape. I debated whether to feel around the walls or just sit there and wait for help, but what help could possibly come when no one knew where I was? If Owen wasn't the Yowie, then my aunts would find the note and come looking for me.

I only hoped my aunts would find me soon.

I edged a little further away from my original position. Where was this? Was it a basement? We rarely had basements in Australia. I didn't think I was on a boat, because there was no rocking at all. No, I must be in a basement, or a cellar. Yes, that was more like it, a wine cellar. Could I be at the winery? And if so, did that mean Lucas O'Callaghan was the Shifter, after all? And what did he intend to do with me?

I didn't have long to wait until my eyes adjusted. It made me think it was probably a vampire ability, an ability to see in the dark.

It wasn't a wine cellar after all; it was a small room with, as I'd guessed, brick walls and a concrete floor. Cartons lay carelessly tossed to one side, covered with cobwebs and dust. A huge huntsman spider ran up the wall, close to me. I recoiled and jumped away, and then tripped over something at my feet.

I looked down and was horrified to see a body.

I bent down, and could make out Linda's features. Blood was trickling from her hair. I held my breath for what seemed like an age, patting her cheek, lightly at first, and then harder. "Linda, are you okay?" I said over and over again.

She groaned, and her eyelids flickered.

"Thank goodness!" I said aloud.

"Pepper? What happened?" She tried to sit up.

I restrained her. "Linda, lie down. Your head's bleeding. Stay still, you might have concussion."

"What happened?" she said again.

"Someone hit me on the head, too. I have a huge lump." I touched it once more, and then drew my fingers away, looking for blood. There wasn't any, but it still hurt horribly. "We're locked in some sort of cellar. I didn't see him, but I'm pretty sure it was Owen."

"Owen." Her voice was weak.

I nodded, but then realised she couldn't see me.

"Owen was the last person I saw before I was hit," she said.

I was right, after all. Owen was a Shifter, and my aunts had captured his accomplice brother.

I looked round for something that could act as a pillow, but came up blank. I figured it would probably be covered with red back spiders, anyway. Linda once more struggled to sit up. "Are you sure you shouldn't lie down?"

"No," she said, her voice stronger.

I helped her sit against a wall. "Do you remember what happened to you?"

She groaned, but then answered readily enough. "I called the winery to ask if I could visit, but they said they were shut to the public for a while. I told them I was an old friend of Henry's, so they said I could visit."

Her voice degenerated into a coughing fit. "I'm afraid I don't have a bottle of water or anything," I said. "Don't try to talk."

"It's okay. I was supposed to go tomorrow because they were understaffed today, but I got impatient and drove out there. I caught the sergeant lighting the fire, but he saw me, too."

"What happened then?"

"I don't remember. I just remember waking up here, and I was relieved he hadn't killed me."

Not yet, I thought. Aloud I said, "Maybe he wants information from us?"

Linda faded out of consciousness.

The door rattled. I knew I was about to come face-to-face with my attacker.

CHAPTER 21

I pushed myself back against the wall, afraid. If only I could remember how I had moved swiftly when the snake struck, because that was a good defensive move. The only thing was, I hadn't done it deliberately.

I saw to my dismay that the door was heavy and barred. Worse still, my captor was standing on the other side.

"Owen! Why did you lock me in here?"

"Where's my brother?" he snapped. He seemed an entirely different person, menacing, brooding. His expression was ominous.

"Your brother?" I said, doing my best to sound puzzled.

"Don't play dumb with me. I know you vampires have my brother captive."

"Vampires?" I echoed, once more faking my astonishment.

"I saw you move when the snake struck at you," he said. "Only a vampire has that speed. I hadn't suspected you up until then, Pepper. Now tell me where my brother is, and I'll let you go."

I did not believe him. I did not believe that he would let me go, not in the slightest. I knew what he intended to do to Linda, too. What's more, I didn't know how successful a vampire would be in a fight against a Shifter, and I didn't want to find out. After all, I had no idea how to control any of my nascent abilities. Gosh, the only ability I knew I had was the fast movement, and I had no idea how to replicate that.

He growled, so I thought I should speak. "As you know, I've just moved to town. I arrived only moments before that body fell through the roof. I don't know what's going on. I told you, I hadn't visited my aunts for years, and my parents didn't like them."

He appeared to be thinking it over. I hoped he would think I didn't realise I was a vampire, but that was a slim hope. Finally, he spoke. "No matter,

I'm holding you to ransom. I'm going to make an exchange for Ethan, my brother. In case you haven't figured it out for yourself, I destroyed that note you wrote for your aunts."

"But why?" I asked. It didn't make sense. He said he'd only known I was a vampire when I moved quickly away from the snake, but he had destroyed the note prior to that.

"I thought Marius was the vampire who'd captured my brother," he said, narrowing his eyes, "and Linda Williams was in it with him, only I hit her too hard and she wasn't talking. I caught her following me. I thought you would lead me to where Marius was holding Ethan. If that was the case, then I'd have to do away with you, so that's why I destroyed the note. I had no idea at the time that you were involved in my brother's disappearance."

"But I wasn't," I said, my voice sounding small to my ears.

"I didn't know there were other vampires in Lighthouse Bay, or I never would've moved here."

"Other vampires?" I asked him.

"Your aunts, whatever they really are," he said flatly. "I knew about Henry Ichor, of course, and his Witches' Brew."

273

"Is that why you killed the wine scientist?" I asked him. I was choosing my words carefully, in case Linda had regained consciousness.

He made a rude, snorting sound. "You're a bit slow on the uptake, aren't you? Of course that's why my brother and I killed Talos Sparkes."

"Did you kill Henry Ichor, or was that really an accident?"

"Of course it wasn't an accident!" he said with derision. "Ethan put a bomb in Henry's car, and he ended up over the side of a steep cliff in northern India."

I didn't want to irritate him, but I had to know. "Why did you kill Henry Ichor and the wine scientist?"

He sighed as if I were particularly stupid. "The Witches' Brew, of course. It's exported to you vampires all over Australia. It heightens your powers."

I still was none the wiser. "I don't get it," I said honestly. "I don't believe in mythical creatures," I added for Linda's benefit, "but why would you care if vampires have heightened powers?"

"Vampires are always a threat to Shifters," he said.

Something occurred to me. "Do you mean

Shifters in general, or just those Shifters engaged in criminal activity?"

He laughed and pointed at me. "You got it! My brother and I were going to set up a nice little business here. He was buying that car dealership, and we were going to transport the cocaine in the cars. Lighthouse Bay is half way between Sydney and Brisbane, so we can do a good trade in cocaine. Police never look at small towns for this sort of thing; they always concentrate on the Gold Coast, places like that. There are no other Shifters in Lighthouse Bay, so it was ideal. We just had to make sure vampires didn't interfere. There are so many vampires in law enforcement, mostly lawyers."

"But surely the Ambrosia Winery isn't the only one that makes the Witches' Brew?"

Owen rolled his eyes. "It's the only one that makes it in decent quantities. It's the most notable winery of its kind. There are some wineries at Margaret River in Western Australia, and wineries in the Hunter Valley as well as in Victoria that make the Witches' Brew as well, but the Ambrosia Winery is by far the best."

"Gosh, how many vampires are in Australia?" I said in shock, more to myself than to him.

"You really are new to all this, aren't you?" he said, baring his teeth.

I recoiled. "You could say that." I didn't know whether or not he intended to kill me, but I thought I was safe so long as my aunts had his brother. "Let me get this straight: you and your brother killed Henry Ichor and the wine scientist to stop them making the Witches' Brew?"

"Yes, I've already explained that to you, Pepper." His tone held a considerable degree of disdain.

"But wouldn't there be a formula for it, like um, a recipe on someone's computer, and wouldn't it be backed up to the Cloud?"

"Thankfully, that's not the case or I would be in rather a pickle." He laughed. "You really don't know, do you?"

"Know what?"

"Vampires have a different skill set, and..." His voice broke off. "How can I explain this? You can't *learn* to make Witches' Brew. There is no formula for Witches' Brew. People are born with the knowledge."

"You're kidding!"

He shot me a long hard look, probably to see if

I was faking my ignorance, only my ignorance was entirely genuine.

"It's an ability someone's born with. You can't learn to make the Witches' Brew. Someone is born with the knowledge, and they can't tell anyone else how to make it. They do it by intuition, and they have to oversee the process in person."

A wave of irritation flooded over me. I was learning more about vampires in a few moments with my attacker, a Yowie Shifter, than I had from my aunts, though to be fair, they *had* mentioned the genetic ability to make Witches' Brew. I just hadn't taken it all in at the time. "But the wine scientist? You're saying he wasn't really a wine scientist at all?"

Owen made a strange sound like a grunt, and I hoped he wasn't in the process of transforming into a Yowie. "No of course not, that's just what they called him. He was a witch-vampire, just like Henry Ichor."

"And is Lucas O'Callaghan a wine scientist, too?" I asked him.

"Of course not," Owen said again, "or he would've been working in the business already. No, he's just a mundane person who's inherited a winery that he thinks is selling mundane wine." He laughed in a guttural manner, and this time I truly was afraid he was shifting. "And real wine scientists don't actually have anything to do with Witches' Brew; that's just a cover. He was Henry's nephew."

I pretended I didn't know. "Lucas's cousin?"

"From the other side of the family," Owen said. "That was clearly the vampire side." He was speaking reasonably, as if we were simply two acquaintances having a conversation about the weather, or some such thing.

"So by killing Henry Ichor and the wine scientist or whatever he really was," I said, "you have pretty much shut down the making of Witches' Brew at the Ambrosia Winery?"

"That's right."

"You're not going to go around Australia killing all the makers of Witches' Brew, are you?" I said, worried.

"The rest are all small wineries, nothing to worry about," he said dismissively. "I've already told you that. Ambrosia is the main winery, and their line of Witches' Brew was immeasurably superior to anything else produced in Australia. You really are quite the ignorant one, aren't you!"

"So Marius Jones isn't a Shifter?"

Owen did not respond to that. "I'm going to go

and have a little word with your aunts. I'm going to make arrangements to trade you for Ethan."

I was going to make a half hearted attempt to say that my aunts didn't have his brother, but I thought it too late for subterfuge. He already seemed to have a good idea of the facts. "Why is Linda Williams here?"

"She saw me, of course. You helped me by saying Linda held a grudge, so it will look like she started the fire. No one will hear you if you scream, so don't even bother trying," he continued. "But if it makes you feel better, go for it. I live out of town, and no one comes out this way. If you scream, only the goannas will hear you. But go ahead if you want to—knock yourself out." With that, he uttered a guttural laugh and left.

Once again, I was left in the darkness, but once more, I could see easily. I looked around for anything I could use. Clearly, he hadn't intended to take any prisoners on short notice, because the room was a mess.

The first thing I noticed was that there was no window, not even a small space crack that I could call through, but if he was telling the truth about being out on the edge of town, no one would hear me, anyway.

I looked through the barred door and saw a big metal key hanging on a hook on the far wall. Surely that couldn't be the key to unlock the door? I had seen so many movies where people found something in a prison cell and threw it over the key on the far wall, and managed to drag the key towards them. I had always wondered why someone would be silly enough to leave a key there.

But then again, where else would he put it? It was a huge metal key, so he could hardly put it on his key chain.

"Linda, are you awake? There's a huge key hanging on that far wall."

Linda muttered something incomprehensible, but I was pleased to see she was still sitting up, propped against the wall.

I kept looking around the room for something I could use. There were some old bricks, so I picked one up. It had a fat red back spider on it, so I screamed and dropped it. The spider scurried off. I cautiously picked up all the bricks, first examining them one by one for the small yet highly venomous red back spiders, and took them over to the door. I planned to throw them at the key and see if I could dislodge it, but what I really needed was a broom or rake.

Sadly, there was no such implement in the room. There were plenty of cartons, so I searched through them all. They looked like they had been there for years—the *Australian Women's Weekly* magazine, several fishing magazines, and cartons of children's toys. I was worried about my aunts. I knew they weren't elderly ladies, but then, Owen clearly knew that, too. Plus he had the element of surprise on his side. They probably didn't even know I had gone.

I kept searching through boxes, finding more dust than anything else. Finally, I hit the jackpot, a piece of rope. This was an old, inflexible rope, but it was better than nothing. I crossed to the bars and poked my hands through them, one hand holding the brick. I threw the brick as hard as I could against the hook holding the key. It hit it, but the key remained there.

I really needed a long pole to push the key up and over the hook, but I didn't have anything like it, so I threw the next brick. Again, it landed on the hook, and again, the hook stayed upright. I wondered just how far into the concrete wall the hook had been screwed. Probably a long way, by the look of it.

I picked up the last brick and flung it as hard as

I could against the hook. This time, the hook partially dislodged from the wall and hung down at an angle.

"Finally, I'm getting somewhere!" I said to Linda. However my high spirits deflated when I realised I didn't have any more bricks. I looked back through the boxes for something else. It wouldn't take much to dislodge that hook.

I found some cricket balls, and took them over to the door. With my first throw, I missed entirely. I aimed again, and scored a direct hit this time, but the hook did not so much as shudder.

I threw the next ball harder, and managed, more by luck than by skill, to hit the hook. To my delight, the key fell to the ground. Now I just had to move the key over to the barred door.

I grabbed the heavy rope. I pushed it through the bars and tried to throw it as far as I could, but it was a thick stiff rope and not flexible in the slightest. I tied a knot at the end—a difficult feat given its thickness—coiled it up, hung onto the end and then flung it as far as I could. I missed, but it had made the distance, so I knew I was on the right track.

"Is that a car outside?" Linda said urgently. "Hurry!"

Was Owen coming back for me to make the swap? I coiled the rope and threw it urgently.

This time, it landed directly on top of the key. I jumped with delight. I carefully pulled the rope towards me, and the key started to move. I held my breath. I pulled the rope once more, but it slipped over the top of the key.

I could see the problem at once. While the floor inside the basement was concrete, the area outside was flagstones, and the key had lodged itself in between the flagstones.

Although it was counterintuitive, I realised I had to push the key back away from me.

I flung the rope once more, and this time, achieved what I wanted. The key did leave the groove between the flagstones, but I had thrown the rope too hard and the key landed against the far wall.

"Pepper, someone's coming! He's back!"

I made one last desperate attempt to throw the rope again.

It landed on the key and I managed to pull it in such a way to avoid the groove in which it had lodged on my previous attempt. Once more, the rope slid off, but I was fairly sure I could reach the key. I bent down, but it was just out of range.

I lowered myself to the floor, and pushed my shoulder as hard as I could into the bars. My fingers closed around the key ring. I pulled it towards me.

After what seemed an age, but was only moments, I had the key in my hand, and inserted it in the lock on the other side of the door. It didn't turn easily. In fact, it took me a significant and frustrating amount of time to open the door, and I wasn't helped by Linda urging me to hurry.

I opened the door and stepped gingerly into the anteroom. There was only one way out, up the stairs to the right. "Linda, come on."

"You go and get help," she said. "I don't think I can make it."

I took the steps two at a time. At the top of the stairs, I flung the door open, momentarily blinded by the bright daylight. I took a step forward right into a hard, muscular body.

Someone gripped my arms.

I looked up into the face of Lucas O'Callaghan.

CHAPTER 22

I acted without thinking. I drew back my leg, and then kicked him in the shin as hard as I could.

Lucas doubled over with a cry of pain. I made to run past him, but his hand shot out and took hold of my arm. "I've come to rescue you."

I struggled, but he was too strong. He seized my arms and pulled me back to him. "How do I know you're not working with Owen?" I asked against his chest.

He looked down at me and hesitated before speaking. "Because if I was, I wouldn't pretend to rescue you. I would fling you over my shoulder and toss you back in wherever he was holding you."

I pulled away and looked up at him, blinking in the bright sunlight. His words made sense.

His eyes looked me up and down. "Did he hurt you?"

"Not too much," I said, realising that I'd had a lucky escape. "He hit me over the head with something." My hand moved to the lump on my head. I winced as I touched it; it was a nasty lump. Tears pricked at my eyes.

"Hey," Lucas said. "Hey. It's okay. Pepper, look at me." He placed a hand beneath my chin and lifted my head, so that he and I were staring into each other's eyes.

He has such lovely eyes, I thought. "Oh dear," I whispered, trying to keep my knees from buckling.

"What did you say?" Lucas tilted his head to the side.

"Fine. I'm fine. I think. Probably."

"You're not fine."

"I'm not?"

"No." I placed a hand on Lucas's chest to keep from falling over. I could feel his warmth through the cotton of his shirt. He did not speak, only looked into my eyes and covered my hand with his own. Before I knew it, I was in his arms, his hands now pressed into the small of my back. I buried my face into his neck and sobbed, shivering as I felt his hands run over my hair.

"I thought he was going to kill me," I murmured.

He pulled me even closer to him. "You're in shock." He cupped my face. I barely had a chance to think before I was gone, lost to the warmth of his hands on my skin and the feel of his lips lightly touching mine. All of a sudden, he broke away.

I was mortified. Did he think I had wanted to kiss him? Granted, I *had* wanted to, but surely it was just the shock of being kidnapped. I suddenly came to my senses. "Linda Williams is down in there." I pointed to the way I had come. "She has a head injury."

Lucas hurried past me. By the time I reached the cellar, he was helping Linda out. "I feel a bit better knowing Owen isn't about to kill me now," she said to me.

"He could be back any minute," I pointed out.

Lucas guided Linda into the car—Aunt Agnes's blue Mazda—and helped her into the back seat, where she lay down as best she could in the cramped space. Before we drove off, Lucas called the police and told them he needed an ambulance for Linda. The ambulance was going to take a while, so they said they would meet us at Mugwort Manor.

It was only when we were driving that I asked him, "How did you know where to find me?" I looked straight ahead, embarrassed.

"Your aunts came looking for you," he said. "They said you were missing. They were distraught, given that there had already been one murder at Mugwort Manor." He shot me a sideways look. "And I've been doing a bit of detective work. My uncle mentioned Sergeant Carteron's brother, Ethan, to me some time ago. He said Ethan had a personal grudge against him, but he didn't say what. Ethan has a long history of violence."

"How do you know that?" I asked him.

"I have friends in the police force," he said. "When you went missing, I thought a good place to start looking for you would be Sergeant Carteron's house."

Before he could say any more, I clapped my hand over my mouth. "He's headed straight to my aunts! He thinks they captured his brother."

"Why would he think that?" Lucas asked me. His tone sounded innocent enough, but I didn't know if there was more to it.

"He last saw his brother when they both

murdered Talos Sparkes," I said. "He confessed to that. He said his brother put an explosive device in your uncle's car when he was in northern India."

I heard Lucas's sharp intake of breath.

"He must've left his brother behind when he killed Talos Sparkes," I said. "I suppose he rushed off because he knew my aunts would call in the murder, and he didn't see his brother after that, so he figured my aunts had caught him. You know, given it all happened at Mugwort Manor."

"But that makes no sense," Lucas said evenly. "Even assuming your aunts had somehow managed to catch a murderer, why wouldn't they hand him over to the police?"

I nodded vigorously. "Exactly! Either Owen's gone completely mad, or there's something he didn't want to tell me." It sounded lame to me, but I hoped Lucas bought it. "I've got to call the police."

Lucas pulled his phone from his pocket and handed it to me. "Call them back. I have Detective Anderson's number in my contacts."

I called Detective Anderson, and mercifully, he answered at once. I told him that Owen had kidnapped me and locked me in the basement in his home. I told him that Owen was headed for my aunts, thinking that they had his brother, Ethan, and Owen had confessed to me that they had killed both Henry Ichor and Talos Sparkes. I told him he must hurry to Mugwort Manor, because Owen was headed there now, convinced that my aunts were holding his brother hostage.

Mercifully, the detective didn't ask me any questions, but said he would speak to me later.

I cast a quick glance at Lucas. "I hope they get there in time."

Lucas didn't respond. The car was travelling fast, but I wasn't scared of the speed. I was only worried what Owen would do to my aunts.

When we reached Mugwort Manor, the detective's car was outside, as were two marked police vehicles. Lucas and I hurried up the flagstone path. A uniformed officer tried half-heartedly to stop us entering the house. "Linda Williams is in the car," Lucas said. "She has a head injury, and the ambulance is on its way." The officer nodded and rushed over to the car.

I was at the top of the flagstone path when I heard the ambulance siren, but I hurried inside. I was overwhelmed with relief to see that all my aunts appeared unharmed.

Both Owen and the man I now knew to be

Ethan lay on the floor, unconscious. "What happened?" I said to no one in particular.

Aunt Dorothy hurried over to me and enveloped me in a giant bear hug. "Valkyrie, are you all right? We were so worried."

"Owen kidnapped me," I said, once again fighting back the tears. "I think he might be doing drugs or something. He confessed to murdering Talos Sparkes and Henry Ichor, and he said he left his brother here after he murdered Talos. He thought you were holding his brother here in an attempt to blackmail him. He wanted to trade me for him." I wiggled my eyebrows as I said it.

"How strange," Aunt Agnes said. "We heard someone ringing the doorbell and we thought it was you, Valkyrie. When we opened the door, both men rushed inside. They didn't tell us what they wanted, because they were yelling at each other and then I'm afraid they became silent."

"Did they hurt you?" I asked in horror.

"No, dear, they were punching each other," Aunt Dorothy said. "We didn't know what to do, so we called the detectives. By the time they came, the men had punched each other so much that they knocked each other out."

"Oh." I realised that of course the aunts had invented the whole story. It was obvious that they had somehow managed to overpower Owen, and then brought out the other Shifter as a cover for the police.

"So none of you were hurt?" I asked them.

They all shook their heads.

"We'll have to take your statements later," Detective Anderson said. "All you ladies have had the most horrible shock, so I think you should all sit down and have a nice cup of tea first." He gestured to the living room. "Constable Walker, would you make these ladies some tea?"

The constable hurried in the direction of the kitchen. I felt sorry for her, given that her police partner was a Yowie Shifter. Not that she knew that, of course. I hesitated. Or did she? There was more to this town than I had ever suspected. I would have to keep a close eye on that woman, especially as she still could not keep her eyes off Lucas. I was only glad he didn't offer to help her in the kitchen.

"How did he kidnap you?" Detective Banks asked me. "That is, if you're up to talking yet."

I nodded. "When I realised that Marius Jones was robbing the house, I called Owen. After the police arrested Marius, I told Owen that I'd seen Marius acting furtively in the sand dunes, and he asked me to show him where. He overpowered me, and the next thing I knew, I woke up in the wine cellar on what I assume was his property."

Detective Anderson came into the room, talking on his phone. "Would that be the wine cellar with a large barred door?"

I nodded. "Yes, that's the room he locked me in. He kept the key on the opposite wall—it was a huge metal one, an antique, I suppose, like the door. I threw a few bricks at the key hook to break it and some cricket balls, too, and then I managed to dislodge the key and drag it to me with a heavy rope."

"That was very resourceful of you," Lucas said. I thought I detected a note of admiration in his voice, but that might have been wishful thinking. Perhaps it was simply sarcasm.

"And then Lucas found me," I said, my face heating as I remembered the almost-kiss.

"Do you have any idea why Ethan and Owen Carteron suddenly turned up at your house?" Detective Banks asked my aunts.

"No, I didn't know the man was the sergeant's brother until you told us." Aunt Agnes was a picture of wide eyed innocence, and I half believed her, even though I knew what was really going on.

I risked a glance at Lucas. His face was impassive. I wondered if he was swallowing their story, because it sure seemed like the detectives were.

"Was his brother on drugs, too?" I asked them.

Both detectives turned to focus their attention on me. "Drugs?" Banks said. "What do you mean?"

"I just assumed Owen was doing drugs," I said. "He was raving at me and speaking nonsense. What he said didn't make any sense at all, so I figured he was on drugs."

"You may well be right," Banks said. "We'll soon know, once we get the results of the drug screening back."

I saw Agnes and Maude exchange glances, and the corners of their lips twitched. I suspected they had slipped both men something, no doubt as a cover story.

One thing was still puzzling me. "What was that dog hair you found around the tree?"

"Oh that." The detective waved his hand dismissively. "That was from a wolf." The constable had returned, and handed me a cup of tea. I snatched my hand back and she nearly dropped it.

"A wolf, you say? I didn't think there were any wolves in Australia." I clutched my throat in fear. I was thinking of werewolves. Owen and his brother were both Yowie shifters. Did the wolf hair found near the tree mean there were other Shifters, specifically werewolves, in town too?

"Nothing to worry about, Miss Jasper," Detective Anderson said. "It was just a ruse, intended to throw us off the track. Owen and his brother had obviously collected some hair from a zoo and put it there to confuse the forensics tests. It doesn't make any sense, but perhaps the drugs drove them out of their minds."

"They went to some lengths, then," I said, noticing my aunts were avoiding looking at me.

"They did indeed," the detective said, "including how they managed to drag that man to the roof. I know there were two of them, but..." His voice trailed away and he wiped his forehead. "Maybe we'll never know."

My three aunts sat opposite me, sipping tea delicately, looking for all the world like three elderly ladies. They were right; no one would suspect they were up to anything. Society did underestimate elderly ladies—it was the perfect cover.

"I never did trust Sergeant Carteron," I said to no one in particular.

"That was just because he wouldn't let you order dessert," Aunt Agnes said.

"You can never trust a man who doesn't order dessert," I said lightly, feeling some of my courage return. I wanted to have a glass of Witches' Brew, only that wouldn't be appropriate in front of the detectives, and would only serve to make Lucas suspicious. I didn't know how much he knew. The aunts didn't think Lucas was a werewolf or a vampire, but that didn't mean he wasn't.

I wondered what would happen to the Witches' Brew. Owen had said it was by far the superior product in the whole of Australia. Did that mean my aunts would have to import some for our use? Or could we find an Australian winery that made half decent Witches' Brew?

I certainly hoped so. What if there was a shortage of Witches' Brew, and vampires had to go back to biting people? I shuddered.

"Are you all right, Miss Jasper?"

I looked up at Detective Banks. "I was just letting my imagination run away with me," I said truthfully.

"Well then, when you ladies are up to it, we'll take your statements."

"Can I just get cleaned up first, and then my aunts and I will come down to the station?" I asked.

Detective Banks agreed readily enough. I was relieved; my aunts and I needed to get our story straight.

The detectives made to leave, and I was afraid Lucas would question us closely before my aunts and I had time to compare notes. My aunts must have thought so too, because Aunt Agnes stood up. "Off you go, Valkyrie. Hurry, we don't want to keep the nice detectives waiting."

I shot her a grateful look. I hurried out of the room, pausing only to shoot Lucas a surreptitious look. I avoided eye contact, the memory of that almost-kiss still fresh on my mind, and hurried up the stairs. I knew he would likely ask my aunts questions, but I was sure they were more than a match for him. After all, they had been doing this for years, centuries even.

CHAPTER 23

I was sitting in the garden at the back of Mugwort Manor, stroking the black cat. My aunts had prepared cheese and olive platters, and had invited Lucas O'Callaghan for an evening drink. They said it was to thank him for saving me, and although I had pointed out that I had saved myself, they ignored me.

The air was thick. It was a hot evening after all, and a storm was brewing, judging by the black clouds gathering volume at an alarming rate, yet the humidity was low. There were no flies, so that was something to be grateful for. A gentle breeze moved the garish blue umbrella above my head, and I wondered if my aunts had assembled it correctly.

I was in two minds about Lucas coming over.

The time since my arrival had been eventful, to say the least. I wanted to lie on the couch for the rest of the day, eating junk food and drinking Witches' Brew. The police questioning had been easy, considering that my aunts and I had ensured that our stories matched before we had given our statements to the police.

All had gone smoothly. Of course, Owen and his brother were not going to admit that they were Shifters, so they were remaining tight-lipped, or so I had been given to understand.

Aunt Agnes's voice broke me from my thoughts. "I'm so proud of you, Valkyrie, keeping your head and releasing yourself from the prison. You always did say there was something funny about the sergeant."

I nodded, turning my face towards the cool breeze.

"Here comes Mr O'Callaghan now," Aunt Maude said over her knitting.

"Call me Lucas, please," he said.

I fidgeted in my seat. I still felt embarrassed around him, although I told myself that his lips had moved towards mine just as much as mine had moved towards his.

Lucas handed Aunt Agnes a bottle of wine. She

thanked him, and added, "Will the winery have to close now?"

He looked taken aback. "Why would you say that?"

"I meant to say, this is special label wine. I suppose you can't produce any more special label wine, what with your uncle and the wine scientist both murdered."

Lucas took the seat offered to him at the big round table opposite me. "Oh no, that won't be a problem. I'm a wine scientist, too."

"You are?" The words were out before I could stop them. All three aunts shot me a warning look. It could have been worse—had I been drinking wine when he disclosed that little gem, I would've coughed it right up, then and there.

Lucas did not appear to have noticed. "Oh yes, I did a degree in wine science in Queensland."

Oh, so that's what he meant. He meant a normal wine scientist, not a witch-vampire wine scientist. "Uncle Henry left me detailed instructions on how to make the special label wine," he continued. "It was all in his will."

I frowned. The aunts had said that no one would be able to produce Witches' Brew unless that person was actually a witch-vampire. I thought it strange that Henry Ichor had left instructions. Was Lucas lying? I would have to ask my aunts about that later. Meanwhile, they were going about their business, pretending simply to be gracious hosts. They *were* gracious hosts, but I was sure they had an ulterior motive for inviting Lucas for drinks. Maybe they wanted to extract information from him about the wine.

I looked up to see Lucas nodding. "Yes, I'll have to bring one of the first bottles of the new wine I make over to you, and you can tell me if there's any difference," he said.

"I wouldn't be able to tell," Aunt Agnes said. "One wine tastes the same as the other to us, but Valkyrie would be able to give you an opinion. Young people tend to drink more these days, don't they?"

I nodded politely, not really listening. I wondered if Lucas was in fact a witch-vampire, hiding his identity from us. Still, I supposed he had no alternative. After all, he couldn't go around shaking hands with strangers and saying, "Pleased to meet you. I'm a witch-vampire, are you?"

I dismissed that fanciful notion and chuckled. For all I knew he was a werewolf, or some other sort of Shifter. I looked up to see everyone looking at me. "What are you laughing at, Valkyrie?" Aunt Agnes asked me.

"Nothing," I said with a smile. "I was just thinking how nice it was to be here, relaxing in the evening, smelling the salt air and drinking good wine with friends. Oh, I mean with friends who are my aunts, and a guest." I didn't want Lucas to think I considered him my friend. And he wasn't a friend —he was simply an object of desire and a rather rude, conceited man at that. I pulled my eyes away from his broad shoulders and that stubble running across his handsome jaw.

"And a cat," Lucas added, bending down to stroke the cat.

I jumped and tore my eyes from him. "I'll have to give her a name," I said. "I can't keep calling her *The Cat*."

"She already has a name," Aunt Dorothy said.

I looked up sharply. "You never told me that!"

"Didn't I?" she said absently, and then took a sip of wine.

"Well, what's her name?" I prompted.

"How should I know?" Aunt Dorothy sipped more wine. "She hasn't told me," she said after an interval.

"But you said..." I stopped and scratched my head.

"She surely has a name, but she hasn't told us what it is," she said.

I leant back in my seat. I thought Lucas was trying not to laugh, but did he ever laugh? The man was an enigma. I wondered if my aunts actually were eccentric, or whether it was all part of their act.

Still, I considered that it didn't matter. My aunts were family. Even if they were centuries older than I was, we had a bond. I was happy and secure for the first time in years. Sure, I was a vampire and my aunts were vampires, but I wouldn't let a little thing like that worry me. I was certain I would be happy in Lighthouse Bay.

NEXT BOOK IN THIS SERIES

WITCHES AND WINE BOOK 2

Witches' Secrets

Pepper Jasper thinks she's had more shocks than anyone should have in one lifetime, yet more sinister secrets lie in wait for her. And when one of the guests is murdered, Pepper discovers danger is closer than she thought.

Can Pepper remain hidden from those who wish her harm?

Lucas O'Callaghan is hiding something, and Pepper is determined to find out what it is.

As trouble brews, Pepper races to sift through the clues, and does her best to stay alive.

ABOUT MORGANA BEST

USA Today bestselling author Morgana Best survived a childhood of deadly spiders and venomous snakes in the Australian outback. Morgana Best writes cozy mysteries and enjoys thinking of delightful new ways to murder her victims.

www.morganabest.com

Made in the USA
Monee, IL
03 May 2021

67600396R00184